KISS OF STEELE
THE ROYAL OCCULT BUREAU
BOOK 9

BARBARA RUSSELL

All rights reserved.

No part of this publication may be sold, copied, distributed, reproduced or transmitted in any form or by any means, mechanical or digital, including photocopying and recording or by any information storage and retrieval system without the prior written permission of both the publisher, Oliver Heber Books and the author, Barbara Russell, except in the case of brief quotations embodied in critical articles and reviews.

PUBLISHER'S NOTE: This is a work of fiction. Names, characters, places, and incidents either are the product of the author's imagination or are used fictitiously. Any resemblance to actual persons, living or dead, business establishments, events, or locales is entirely coincidental.

Kiss of Steele Copyright 2025 © Barbara Russell

Cover art by Dar Albert at Wicked Smart Designs

Published by Oliver-Heber Books

0 9 8 7 6 5 4 3 2 1

ONE

SOMEWHERE IN THE ATLANTIC OCEAN, 1887

FEELING SICK ON A BOAT—PARDON, ship—is an utterly undignified affair.

I'd been casting up my accounts from the moment my unfortunate journey on the *Steam Ship Florentia* had started. When I'd left Southampton a few days ago, I could have never imagined that going on a cruise could be so painful. I'd been confused and suspicious about the trip but also thrilled and curious. How wrong I'd been.

And people went on a cruise to take a holiday?

We'd been cruising all the way down to France, and now the ship was sailing through... I didn't have the foggiest idea where. All around me was an endless blue expanse that moved, lifted, and lowered, lifted and lowered. Oh, Lord.

A new wave of nausea caught me. Gripping the

handrail, I leant over the side of the deck and emptied my stomach into the endlessly grey view of the Atlantic Ocean. Just watching the water shifting, the sunlight glinting off the waves, and the white foam bubbling made me feel sick all over again.

Thank goodness that corner of the deck was empty. The SS *Florentia* was a monstrous ship, like a village floating on the sea. The passengers—those who weren't afflicted by seasickness and headaches and didn't wish to die—enjoyed the many forms of entertainment on board, from violin concerts to dance performances and card games. The last thing I wanted was to have a witness to my rather unladylike state. One couldn't feel sick with abandon in front of an audience.

My dark-blonde hair flapped wildly over my cheeks, adding a new layer of discomfort, but I was too weak to gather the long tendrils into a decent chignon. My dress was a mess of wrinkles and stains of dubious origin. Blazes, I'd even lost a button of my shirt somewhere. I could almost hear my mother's horrified comments.

Monia! Compose yourself.

Yes, my name was Monia, short for Sanctimonia. No, not in the sanctimonious, holier-than-thou sense, but in the 'symbol of purity' sense. Purity my foot. I didn't feel pure at all in my current state.

Another sea wave crushed against the hull with a deafening thud. At least it sounded deafening to my poor ears. The deck shifted up and down, and I gripped the handrail harder. Or tried to. Energy had been leaching out of me for the past few days. My legs trembled as I fought to stay upright. But fighting required too much effort. Sod it. I was going to collapse on the deck and stay there. Dignity be darned. Maybe Poseidon would have mercy on me and sweep me away. If I was lucky, I was going to pass out.

I had barely time to release the handrail and let gravity do the rest before a thick, strong arm coiled around my waist and supported me.

"Careful, missus," a deep, slightly raucous voice said close to my ear.

Oh, no. Not *him*. Not now. Not my chaperone!

Groaning inwardly, I gazed up and wished I hadn't. There he was.

Mr Rennie Steele was staring at me with both pity and concern. I wasn't the type of woman to swoon over a gentleman. Most of the time. No sir. But he had a rough, wild type of beauty I admired but didn't make me faint. He had very broad shoulders, lots of muscles, and a harsh jaw. Overwhelmingly strong. His large green eyes were pretty. Intense and charming when they wanted to be. Every time he gazed at me, a little shiver of fear made me quiver. Mr Steele frightened me. I had no problem admitting it.

Slender men with the long and elegant fingers of a pianist were less alarming to me. Rennie's hands were calloused with tiny scars marring the knuckles, and so strong they could snap someone's neck. He looked like one of those bare-knuckle pugilists who thrived in London's underworld. His nose had definitely been broken at least once, judging by its crooked shape.

"I'm fine," I croaked out, wishing to feel sick alone. Self-pity worked much better when I was alone.

"No, you aren't. You don't look fine." His Cockney accent was so thick I could scrub the deck with it.

Why had my parents chosen him as my chaperone instead of an old lady? In fact, why had they sent me here? It wasn't the first time I'd asked myself those questions. My parents and Rennie had been of no help in answering them.

Ten days ago, I'd convinced my parents to let me go to a magnificent ball at one of my friends' houses. Music, champagne, handsome gentlemen, and solid, firm ground underneath my feet. Heaven. My parents had yielded to my request, and I'd hugged them both, happy.

You might find a good suitor. Someone you like, Mother had said.

And I'd found someone! A handsome, sophisticated prince from Rochenstein, a small principality in Central Europe. His name was Sandrosarkbach, and he was perfect. His long midnight hair, blue eyes, pale skin, and willowy body of a dancer had mesmerised me. Admittedly, his name wasn't easy to pronounce. I didn't think I could say it out loud without stammering. The 'Sandro' part was easy, but the last one sounded like my grandfather when he had a coughing fit after he snuffed tobacco. Anyway, Sandro had seemed to be mesmerised by me as well, which had surprised me. I wasn't a wallflower, but I wasn't the type of lady who attracted men's attention, either.

We'd danced and talked for hours. And he'd understood me so well. He'd stolen my heart, paying me a lot of compliments, telling me about the challenges of being a prince, and letting me talk about everything I liked. When he'd asked me to take a stroll in the garden, I'd accepted his invitation. We'd sat on a marble bench under the moonlight, our fingertips brushing against each other, heads leaning closer, and hearts pounding. He'd been about to kiss me. But it'd been the moment when things had started to go horribly wrong.

Mother had spotted me and let out a scream that could have rivalled the police's siren. Sandro had fled like a wanted pirate, and I couldn't blame him. Mother had suffered a complete breakdown. Hysteria had taken her. She'd screamed that her heart was breaking and I was killing her, I was an irresponsible, reckless woman, and I had no idea what trouble I'd put myself in.

Hadn't I been doing what she'd asked me? Finding a husband? And a prince at that! But no. She'd cried and despaired, accusing me of being a silly woman and crying for help. Then Father and she had ordered me to pack my belongings and take a cruise to tour the Mediterranean Sea with Rennie as my chaperone. Odd. At first, I hadn't understood how a cruise in the company of a man, who wasn't one of my relatives, could be a punishment for my so-called lascivious behaviour. But now I did. I so did.

The cruise was sheer torture. The company dreadful. The worst punishment ever.

"Let me go," I said, stepping back from Rennie's embrace.

His jaw clenched, causing a tendon in his neck to stand out. "All right. Just don't fall into the sea. I don't want to dive into the water to rescue you."

No missus or Miss Fitzwilliam. "I have no intention—" A new fit of retching cut me off. I leant over the handrail and did what I'd been doing every cursed day for the past week. Practice didn't make it any easier.

"Here. Let me help." Rennie brushed my hair from my face and held it away from my heated cheeks. How he could drop every 'h' in his speech was a mystery.

"Don't look at me," I said, coughing and spitting.

A raucous laugh rumbled out of him as he held me up and put a comforting hand on my forehead. "Why not? You're pretty."

Somehow, those ill-timed words stopped the nausea. I turned towards him, ready to face the sea again if another wave of sickness took me over. I was about to tell him his comment was inappropriate, especially since we were alone, but what I said was, "Do you think I'm pretty?" Because I wasn't sure I was, what with my matted hair, green skin, and the stink of seasickness.

I wouldn't consider myself stunning, but I knew how to enhance my good traits. With the right dress, hairstyle, and a bit of make-up, I could make an impression. The fact Sandro had been so stunned by me proved it, and surely, even our witty conversation had charmed him. But with Rennie, I hadn't worn anything flattering, taken care of my hair properly, or talked much to him. The latter not for lack of trying. He simply replied with a 'yes' or 'no' to my questions and never started a conversation.

Also, on those rare occasions when we talked, I always asked him about my parents' strange behaviour, and he became silent, refusing to discuss the subject. But wasn't a cruise in the company of a pugilist more damaging to my reputation than a kiss from a prince?

He rummaged through the pocket of his grey suit and produced a large handkerchief with a tartan motif. "Yes, I do think you're pretty," he said, wiping my mouth.

"What are you doing?" Embarrassment was about to kill me. I snatched the handkerchief and hid my face behind it. "I can clean up myself, thank you. I'm not a child."

"Never thought you were, missus." He searched his pocket again and took out a glass vial. "You should try this."

I peered up at the glass vial containing a green liquid. "What is it?" I asked, tilting my head up to stare at his face.

He glanced around before answering. "Something for the sickness. You'll feel better in a moment, but you must take only one drop."

"What's in it?" There was no label on the vial, and I knew better than to trust a stranger offering me a supposedly miraculous potion. What if he wanted to drug me? Although, I'd been so out of sorts lately that, if he'd wanted to take advantage of me, he would have had a dozen occasions.

He scrubbed his unshaven chin. "I don't know. Herbal things. Nothing poisonous. I take it regularly."

"Do you suffer from seasickness too?"

"No."

"Then why do you take it?"

He lifted a shoulder. "As a tonic. To become stronger." For a split second, a smile played on his lips, as if he were enjoying a private joke. "Trust me. It works for seasickness too. It's a cure-all."

As my stomach roiled with nausea again, I admitted defeat and took the vial. But he didn't release it.

"Only one small sip." His eyebrows arched, giving him a menacing look. As if he needed it.

"Fine. Fine." I was ready to try anything at that point.

A faint scent of mint wafted from the vial when I pulled out the stopper. Before another fit of retching started, I swallowed a small sip. The flavours of bay leaves and pepper tickled my taste buds and stung my tongue. The green liquid left a refreshing trail down my throat to my stomach. I held my breath, waiting for the sick feeling to strike again. But nothing came. No, something did come. Sweet relief. The constant ache that had tormented my belly was gone. The headache vanished. The sour taste in my mouth disappeared. I could even breathe more deeply. My mind cleared.

"Good Lord. This potion is wonderful." I studied the

magical vial in the sunlight. "Why didn't you offer it to me earlier?"

"I did." Scowling, he took the vial from my hand. The rough pad of his thumb brushed my skin, reminding me—by contrast—of Sandro's soft, delicate fingers.

Then Rennie's words sank in. "You offered it to me?"

"More than once. You never replied. In fact, you told me to leave you alone, which I did."

Oh, well. It could be true. I'd been so sick that, if he'd asked me something, I doubted I'd heard him. I tugged at my crumpled shirt.

"I apologise for my behaviour. Thank you for your assistance." I tried to regain some dignity, ignoring the fact that my hair was wild and untied and my gown was a nightmare of wrinkled green velvet.

He gave a bow of the head. "You're welcome."

I cleared my throat. "May I keep the vial?"

"No." He slid it into his pocket.

"Why? I'm not going to drink it in one sip."

"When you need it, you'll tell me." His eyes narrowed to slits.

"But—"

He offered me his arm. "I guess you'll want to return to your cabin before dinner."

"Dinner?" At the mention of a meal, I stiffened, worried the nausea might surge again. But my stomach remained quiet. No lurching. No odd noises from my belly. No funny taste in my mouth. "I think I should keep my stomach empty for the moment."

A breeze ruffled his rich chestnut-coloured curly hair, giving him an even wilder look. "You're wrong. You haven't eaten much in the past few days. You need your energy, and trust me, it's better to have food in your stomach when you have nausea. At least you'll have something to puke up if your stomach roils again."

My word, his informal tone would make Mother angry. Again, I wondered why she'd chosen Rennie as my chaperone. Officially, to protect my reputation, he was my cousin, but anyone who saw us together would understand we weren't remotely related.

"I'm not sure I should eat," I said, wringing my hands.

"I insist." He stepped closer, all tall and male, still waiting for me to take his arm.

A hint of fear washed down my spine as his sheer size dwarfed me. I was alone with him. I had no means to communicate with my family unless we docked at a port. He could do whatever he wanted to me.

"I'm not going to kill you and then dump you into the sea, you know?" he said, a wicked smile worthy of a pirate stretching his lips. "I'm here to assist you."

"I was thinking nothing of the sort." I put my hand in the crook of his arm.

"Yes, you were."

As we walked towards the stairs that led below deck and to the cabins, I remained silent. I wasn't used to conversing with gentlemen who were so direct and explicit. I didn't know what to say. No gentleman I knew would be so frank about having guessed my thoughts. Yes, he'd been right, but wasn't pointing out the truth rude? Oh, dear. I rubbed my forehead. I was making no sense.

Now that I wasn't casting up my accounts, I could appreciate the polished wood and golden leaves decorating the walls of the SS *Florentia*. It was a luxurious ship with restaurants, shops, and even a gymnasium. Almost ridiculous. But I'd only seen my cabin and the deck so far.

"Isn't it beautiful?" he asked, pointing at a porthole that opened to a view of the dipping red sun. Orange ignited the waves, turning them into fire-breathing dragons.

I angled towards him. Somehow, I hadn't pictured him as the type of man who would appreciate a sunset.

His eyebrows rose again, disappearing under his thick curls. "What? Can't I like the sunset?"

Drat. What had I said about Sandro understanding me well? It seemed Rennie understood me *too* well. "Actually... Oh, all right." I waved a hand. "I'm guilty as charged. I was thinking that. I guess I should apologise again."

He grinned, his crooked nose twisting further. "Thank you for your honesty."

"You're welcome. From now on, I'm going to tell you exactly what I think about you." I meant it as a joke, but he nodded solemnly.

"Great. I'm curious. What do you think of me?" There wasn't an ounce of humour in the question.

Why had I told him I was going to be honest? I wiped my face again with his handkerchief to buy some time. "I don't know you."

"But you know me enough to make assumptions."

"Don't take that personally. I make assumptions about everyone, even about myself and I'm usually wrong. For example, before leaving for this cruise, I assumed I would be well enough to enjoy the cruise."

He chuckled, and the sound was so charming it made me laugh too.

"So what are your other assumptions about me?" he asked.

"Well, you're a middle-class pugilist who doesn't have a wife or a betrothed."

He resumed walking along the passageway as the red light of the sunset was reflected on the walls. "No wife or betrothed?"

"You wouldn't be here."

"Unless it's my work and you're my charge."

Ha! I wanted to giggle at how easily he gave me some information. "Did my parents pay you to be here?"

"No comment." He clammed up.

I huffed. "I was honest. You should be too."

"I'm not lying. I prefer not to say anything."

"Semantics." I didn't insist. The nausea was gone, but fatigue was weighing me down. Talking tired me out.

We stopped in front of the door to my cabin. I slid my arm out of his. "I'll freshen up and see you in the dining hall."

He gave a curt nod. Something he did a lot.

"See you later." I released a breath when I was alone in my cabin, an odd tingling dancing on my skin.

It was wonderful to wash and change into a fresh dress without groaning with nausea. I winced at my own reflection in the mirror. Pretty? Absolutely not. The sun and the salty air had turned my hair into straw and my skin into a beetroot. The seasickness had made my cheeks gaunt, dried my lips, and given me dark circles around my bloodshot eyes. It took me a good half an hour to tame my tresses into something resembling a chignon and to apply some powder to my face. The rouge wasn't needed. My cheeks and lips were red enough. In fact, I looked almost tipsy. Washing the stink from my body took another half an hour, but afterwards, I was human again.

I chose a white and pink satin dress with small, puffed sleeves and a pink shawl, delicate but elegant. Of course, thanks to my parents' hurry to shove me onto the cursed ship, I didn't have a maid to help me dress.

"Bother." My hands couldn't reach the last buttons on the back of the gown, no matter how much I contorted and strained myself.

Never mind. I covered my back with the shawl. If I kept it around my shoulders, no one would notice the top half of my dress was unbuttoned, and if I didn't move too much, the bodice wouldn't slip down.

I tugged one of my long silk gloves up my hand, pausing over the scar. It was an ugly mark, all uneven edges, and it twisted viciously around my arm. A moment of distraction, an impatient horse, and I'd fallen over a stack of sharp pieces of wood that had stabbed my arm. A choking sensation constricted my throat, which was ridiculous. The incident happened years ago, and after all, nothing had occurred to me aside from the cut on my arm and a scar I could easily hide. It could have been worse. Yet every time I stared at the scar, my breath came out of me in hard pants, and a nagging sensation pricked the back of my neck. I scratched the itchy skin, wincing as I touched the rough, bumpy scar. Would Rennie still think I was pretty if he saw it?

A gasp escaped me when I opened the door. Rennie stood in the corridor—or whatever the name of a corridor on a ship was—his arms folded over his chest and brow furrowed. His forehead smoothed when he raked his gaze over me. It was so quick I wasn't sure he'd been staring at me at all.

"Have you been waiting here for long?" I asked.

His reply was another gaze. "Are you ready?"

"Why did you wait here?" I tugged at my shawl.

He shrugged and offered me his arm again. Annoying man. "Keep an eye on you."

"Is it possible to have a proper conversation with you?" I asked as we strolled along the corridor.

Another shrug. "What would you like to converse about?"

"Well, why are you here, for starters?"

He paused to let a couple of passengers pass. "I'm your chaperone."

"The term 'bodyguard' is more appropriate," I muttered under my breath.

"What do you mean?"

"I know nothing about you. I met you a few days ago in Southampton. Father said you work at his office, but I'm sure I've never seen you. Why would my parents choose you as my chaperone?"

He had the audacity to shrug again with an air of innocence. "That's something you should ask your parents."

"You're impossible."

"Thank you." There was too much amusement in his voice for my liking.

I pressed my lips together and didn't utter a word. Talking with him was pointless. At least I could enjoy the chandeliers and the magnificent brocade curtains in the dining hall. I hadn't noticed how wide and lovely the room was, and I'd admit the view of the sea, shimmering with the moonlight, brought tears to my eyes. For once, emotional tears. A small orchestra played violin music in a corner, and the light from the gas lamps was reflected on the pristine white tablecloths. And the smell! Had the dining room always smelled so delicious? The scent of lemons and lilies filled my nostrils.

As Rennie silently led me to our table right next to a window, I decided that perhaps a good dose of wine would loosen his tongue. It was time to get answers and solve the mystery of my unplanned, utterly horrendous trip.

TWO

RENNIE HAD BEEN RIGHT.

The moment I started eating, my appetite roared back to life. I hadn't realised how hungry I was until I sank my teeth into a delicious slice of roast beef with spinach and roasted potatoes. Everything was spiced to perfection, not too salty or too hot, and the potatoes melted in my mouth, leaving the taste of rosemary and oregano on my tongue. Despite my hunger, I took small pieces of the food. Ladies' manners. Hard habits didn't go away quickly.

"You don't have to impress me," Rennie said, after chomping on a big mouthful of beef. "You must be starving."

I was about to tell him I'd been raised a lady and it was difficult for me to forget my manners when I eyed a waiter carrying a bottle of wine.

"I think you're right." I wiped my mouth with my napkin. "I'd like to have a glass of wine as well."

"No." His forehead furrowed, and the single word rang sharply.

"Excuse me?"

He lowered his knife and leant closer. "I said no."

"And I say you can't order me around." The nerve of this man.

He coughed into his fist. "It's not an order. I was strongly suggesting you not drink wine or any liquor. You took the green serum. You shouldn't drink wine. Green serum and wine don't go well together. In fact, it'd be better if you didn't dance either, just in case the green serum has an unexpected side effect."

"You don't even know what's inside the green serum, but now you're an expert on what I should or shouldn't drink, or what I should do or shouldn't do?" My pathetic plan to convince him to talk was crumbling. "I want a sip of wine." I jutted out my chin.

"Monia." It was a warning. His green eyes flashed.

"I want to dance, and I want a glass of wine." I raised a hand to call a waiter. Yes, yes, I was being childish. But dash it, I blamed him. No one ordered me around, especially since he refused to answer my questions.

I didn't see him moving. One moment, he was sitting and glowering from across the table. The next, he was standing in front of me, blocking my view of the waiter.

"Please, Monia." The corners of his mouth stretched when he said 'please.'

I bit down a comment about the fact that I was Miss Fitzwilliam to him. "Tell me why you are here."

The annoyance in his face—which was likely matching mine—morphed into surprise, then into annoyance again. "Are you blackmailing me?"

"Strongly persuading you to tell me the truth."

"There's no truth to be told."

I lifted my hand and looked past his bulky figure. "Garçon!"

"What are you doing?" He took my hand and lowered it, holding it between his. A strange, fleeting flutter started in the depths of my chest. I wasn't sure it was due to seasickness. "This isn't a hotel or a French restaurant. You can't call the waiter garçon. It's rude."

Ha! Listen who's talking about manners. Besides, he pronounced 'garçon' as 'gross-on,' which made me giggle.

"I'll go to him then." I rose from the stuffed chair in a bold gesture that actually proved to be a disaster. I was half an inch from him when I stood up and he was still holding my hand in a rather intimate fashion.

As close as I was to him, I could see a scar on his neck and another one along his jaw. And blimey, his eyes weren't just green, but a lovely shade of Irish shamrock with golden specks around his large pupils. Unfortunately, in my haste to stand up, my shawl got caught in the ear of the chair and slid off my shoulders. I let out a breath and spun to grab it, but the darn thing slipped to the floor.

"Tarnation." I turned around, showing him my back.

"You're naked," Rennie half-hissed, half-whispered. I could swear his voice sounded all breathy.

"Don't be ridiculous." Cheeks turning into an inferno,

I snatched the shawl and wrapped it around myself before facing him. "Since my parents didn't think of hiring a maid for me, for some absurd reason, I couldn't button my dress fully. But I'm not naked."

Thank goodness the hall wasn't busy, or my moment of hysteria would have had a few witnesses.

His frown deepened. "You could've asked for help." Were his cheeks slightly flushed?

I put a hand on my chest. "From you? Are you out of your mind?" It was outrageous enough to be travelling alone with him. I didn't need him in my cabin, helping me dress and watching my naked body while he fastened buttons and pulled strings.

"Not me." He gritted his teeth. "This ship is full of ladies. Why didn't you ask one of them?"

"Because—"

May the most bloodthirsty hounds of hell chase him. He was right. My mind had conjured up visions of him and me alone and half-naked in my cabin for no reason.

I pulled at the shawl again. "I didn't actually think about that."

"Come." He took my elbow and led me outside, away from the blinding lights of the hall.

"Where are you taking me?"

"You can't dance naked."

"I'm not naked." I shrugged my elbow free. "And didn't you say I shouldn't dance?"

"Let's make a deal." He shut the glass door behind us. The music was cut off as we stood on the deck. A warm wind caressed my skin and carried the scent of the sea. "No wine, but I'll let you dance."

"You'll let me? My, how generous of you," I quipped. "Will you let me have a nightcap too? A quilt against the cold? I'm sure you won't object if I decide to sleep until seven in the morning."

"All right. You've made your point." He held up a hand. "It's for your own good. I'm trying to help."

"While being bossy. Will you tell me something about you?" I asked. "About the job you do for my father? Surely, you can at least tell me that."

He didn't flinch at my harsh tone. "Turn around."

"What for?" I narrowed my gaze.

He heaved a sigh. "So I can button up your dress, and you can have your damn dance."

After a moment of hesitation and scoffing, I turned around. "Honestly. No one has ever talked to me like this before."

"Sorry to hear that," he muttered as he shoved aside the shawl.

"Sorry?"

"Everyone needs honesty. Now stay still."

"That's rudeness, not honesty. You're impossible —" All my bravado froze when his fingers touched the bare skin of my back. With surprisingly infinite gentleness, he worked his way up the dress. Each time he brushed my skin, my breathing came out a little faster. His movements slowed down. His fingertips lingered on my skin a bit longer than necessary with trepidation, as if he were worried I might scream.

He cleared his throat and quickly buttoned up the last button. "There. You're well-covered. Would you like to dance?"

"With you?" I spun around to face him, astonishment giving me extra energy.

Rennie draped the shawl over my shoulders, avoiding my gaze. "If you want to."

Did I want to? Yes, why not? I hadn't had a lot of fun in the past few days, and even though there was something he and my parents were hiding from me, he'd been reasonably kind to me.

His large frame went still as he waited for my answer, and his eyes widened a bit. "I believe it's rude for a lady to refuse an offer to dance."

"Everyone needs honesty," I said.

He chuckled, a sound so deep and rich it brought a smile to my lips. "I deserve it. Is it a no?"

"No." My word, answering as he did was fun.

A corner of his mouth quirked up. He looked more handsome when he smiled. "So it's a yes."

"It is. Let's go." I could always change partners later.

The beam he flashed my way stunned me into silence. I couldn't remember having ever seen him smile like that. Or maybe he had, but I'd been too focused on feeling sick to notice.

The ballroom was right next to the dining hall. Well, one of the ballrooms. The ship had three of them. Ridiculous. The notes of a waltz floated in the air, and excitement sizzled in my chest.

"So, what's your job?" I asked as we walked towards the room.

"I work with your father."

I skidded to a halt. "You promised to give me some answers."

"I didn't." The fabric of his waistcoat stretched over the broad wall of his chest when he inhaled deeply. "Your father is my superior. I work in his unit."

"Are you a soldier?" Father had been in the army, and he was now working at a government office.

Certainly, Rennie looked like a warrior with his hard muscles and sharp gaze. But why would a soldier leave his job to supervise me on a cruise I'd never wanted to take?

He trapped his bottom lip between his teeth, somehow attracting my attention. "More or less."

"What does it mean?"

He resumed walking, leading me to the ballroom. "It means I can't tell you more than that because secrecy is part of the job."

"Fine. Then tell me why my parents chose you, then."

When he pushed open the glass door to the ballroom, the music and chatter hit my senses and distracted me for a moment. The ladies' skirts twirled over the polished floor, and the lights from the chandeliers gleamed over the glossy black dinner suits of the gentlemen. Except Rennie's. He wore his clean but plain grey suit.

"Well?" I prompted him when he didn't answer.

He sighed. "Your parents were worried about you."

"Because of Sandro?"

"Who the hell is Sandro?" He slid an arm around my waist, and I was distracted for the second time as a little shiver crawled up my neck. Blimey, everything he did distracted me.

"Would you please mind your language?" I rolled my eyes. "Sandro is the prince I met at Lady Thompson's ball. He's the reason my parents decided to send me away. I expected to be punished, but they paid a fair amount for this madness, and then they told me you'd come with me."

On the notes of the waltz, he twirled me around, one hand on my waist, the other holding my hand with a gentle touch. I had to admit I'd been with better dancers. Not that Rennie lacked technique, but his feet moved heavily, almost stomping on the floor, and his shoulders were too tense, as if he were ready to fight off an attacker at any moment. Not to mention, he steered me dangerously close to other couples. I didn't want to bump into that lady covered in diamonds and silk. Sandro had held me like a feather and moved with grace and elegance, smiling throughout the dance. Why couldn't I see him again?

"I see," Rennie said, gripping my waist a bit too tightly. "I guess your parents don't approve of Sandro."

"You're an expert at dodging questions and stating the obvious. Sandro is a prince. Mother has been pestering me for months to find a suitable husband. Who can be more suitable than a prince?" My skirts twisted around my legs when Rennie made me turn suddenly. "Besides, I like him, and he likes me. I don't understand why I'm here with you." Oh, dear. I wished my last statement didn't sound like the hiss of a cobra about to strike and wasn't just as poisonous. As much as Rennie was annoying, he didn't deserve my anger. He was doing what my parents had told him to do.

Rennie didn't flinch, though. If my words offended him, he didn't show it.

"Have you thought that maybe your parents know something about Sandro that you don't?" The low baritone of his voice reverberated in my chest as he inched closer.

"I have, but then why didn't they just say so? Why the cloak and dagger? If anything, they made me even more curious about Sandro. If they'd told me he was a scoundrel, I would've forgotten about him." No, I wouldn't. I would have pursued him with more insistence. Every girl needs a scoundrel in her life.

Rennie gave an unconvincing shrug.

Oh, enough of that! I stopped dancing. My skirts twisted again after the abrupt halt. "You know why, don't you?"

"Monia—"

"Just tell me the truth." My voice rose. A few heads turned my way.

He took my shoulders, his strong fingers holding me in place. "I can't. Stop asking me."

The good thing was that he finally admitted there was indeed something he and my parents were keeping from me about Sandro. The bad thing was that he wasn't going to tell me what it was.

"I've had enough." Lifting my chin, I pivoted towards the exit... and promptly tripped on my stupid skirts. How humiliating.

The marble tiles were getting closer as my body threatened to drop to the floor. But Rennie caught me before I hit them.

"Careful." His lips brushed the shell of my ear.

A traitorous tingle started on my skin, even though the quick touch had surely been an accident.

"I don't—" I forgot what I meant to protest about when I turned and found my face inches from Rennie's.

The first thing I noticed was his nose had indeed been broken. A punch, perhaps, or maybe a fall. The second thing I noticed was his scent. It was fresh and soapy, as if he had just finished taking a bath. It had the no-nonsense quality that men, who were used to working with their hands and bodies, had.

Also, the fact he was squashing me against his impossibly hard body didn't escape my notice. None of it changed the situation. He was lying to me. Or rather, he was keeping secrets from me.

I put my hands on his chest and pushed away from him. "I don't want to dance anymore."

"That's a shame," a man with a classy Oxford accent said from behind me. "Because I was about to ask you for a dance, miss." The man flashed a smile that was pure elegance. His blond hair brushed against his cheeks when he bowed, and his sleek dinner suit barely creased. "Please allow me to introduce myself. I'm Mr Edward Marston."

I could only bob a curtsy on my unsteady legs. "Miss Monia Fitzwilliam."

"Monia?" Edward straightened. "What an unusual, beautiful name."

"It's short for Sanctimonia." I probably should stop clarifying it. If Monia sounded odd, Sanctimonia sounded ridiculous, but to his credit, Edward didn't laugh.

"Fascinating," he said in his lovely accent. "Would you care to dance?"

"Miss Fitzwilliam wishes to return to her cabin," Rennie all but growled, stepping next to me.

I arched a brow at him. "So now I'm Miss Fitzwilliam?"

But Rennie wasn't looking at me. His keen gaze was trained on Edward, who was returning the glare.

"I'd love to dance." To break the staring contest, I offered my hand to Edward.

He beamed when he took my hand ever so gently. "Excellent."

"Miss Fitzwilliam," Rennie said through gritted teeth.

"I'll see you later, Mr Steele." I looped my arm around Mr Marston's and glided towards the dancefloor, leaving behind a glowering Rennie.

Oh, Mr Marston was a skilled dancer. He guided me through the waltz with soft steps and elegant moves, knowing exactly when he needed to step to the left or twirl me around. He was a protective dancer without crowding me. Finally, I was enjoying the music and the dance without worrying about tripping. Rennie stood in a corner of the room, scowling at us. Served him right. If he'd only told me the truth.

As we danced, Mr Marston led me away from Rennie and towards the opposite side of the room, even though the dance routine dictated we should move in the other direction. In the manoeuvre, we bumped into another couple, a middle-aged lady with too many feathers in her hair and her stiff companion. Great. What had I said about him being a skilled dancer? Was it a curse that afflicted all the men on board the ship? Or was it me who brought bad luck?

"I beg your pardon," Mr Marston said so charmingly the lady could do nothing but smile in return.

A pretty red-haired girl, who was dancing with a short man, smiled as we twirled close to them. "You're the best dancers I've seen onboard so far," she said. "So elegant."

I gave her a nod. "Thank you."

Mr Marston steered me further down the hall, casting glances at Rennie who was still standing in the same corner.

"Miss Fitzwilliam," he whispered. His face contracted in a tense expression that wiped the smile from my face. "I have something to tell you."

"What?" I craned my neck to glance at Rennie. Perhaps my eagerness to get rid of him had been a tad thoughtless. Uneasiness coiled in my full belly.

"I'm a friend of Sandrosarkbach," Mr Marston said without preamble.

The fluid way he said Sandro's name surprised me almost as much as his words. "Oh, my goodness." My dancing posture slackened, and my elbows dropped to my sides. "Where is he? Why did he leave me? When can I see him again?"

He smiled, eyes brightening. "I'm only a messenger. You'll have the chance to ask him these questions. He's waiting for you in Lisbon where the ship will dock in two days."

A warm shock of surprise ran through me. "Sandro." I'd see him in two days.

Mr Marston threw another glance over his shoulder towards the gloomy figure of Rennie. "I don't need to tell you it would be better if your companion didn't know about the meeting."

No, he didn't need to tell me. But on second thought... "Why?"

He stepped to the left in rhythm with the music. "Again, I'm following Sandro's instructions, but he believes your bodyguard will prevent you from meeting him. Apparently, your parents don't want you to see him."

I was repeating myself, but... "Why?"

Mr Marston heaved a sigh that caused the blond tendrils of his hair to brush against his jaw. "Alas, this is something you must discuss with Sandro himself. I can only tell you this. He's a good man. He would never do anything to harm you or your reputation. Your parents must have taken a dislike to him for some misguided reason."

Mr Marston's words didn't make much sense. In fact, he sounded defensive towards Sandro, as if Sandro had already damaged a lady's reputation. But I wanted answers, so I nodded. "Thank you, Mr Marston. I look forward to seeing Sandro again."

"There's more. Miss Fitzwilliam, you must know there are people who wish him harm."

My breath stilled. "What do you mean?"

"He's a prince and a wealthy, rich man. He has many enemies. Hence the secrecy. You understand, don't you?"

"No, not really."

Impatience flickered over his face. "Sandro will explain everything to you. It's his story to tell. Not mine."

I frowned. The conversation wasn't making much sense. But then again, if I wanted answers, I had to see Sandro.

Rennie shifted his weight. His hard stare was trained on me, and I wondered how I was going to flee from my bodyguard.

THREE

EXCITEMENT WOULDN'T LET me sleep. For the first time since boarding the ship, seasickness wasn't the reason I was awake.

In a couple of days, I'd see my Sandro again and have some answers. Perhaps I read too many novels, but between feeling sick and having nothing to do on board, I'd had a lot of time to think about my predicament. I'd come up with many possible explanations to my parents' odd behaviour.

According to Mr Marston, Sandro was in danger. As the future king of Rochenstein, he must have many enemies. My parents might have decided I needed to stay away from him because his rivals were attempting to take his life. Although, if that was the case, why not tell me? Father served in the army. It wasn't too far-fetched to believe he knew Sandro's life was in danger. I could be in danger too, and if I was going to be honest, a spark of excitement flickered within me.

All my life, I'd been cooped up in the house my parents owned on the outskirts of Oxford. Always controlled by a governess, then a companion, now a bodyguard. I couldn't even ride a horse without having at least two footmen follow me, and I wasn't allowed to ride too far from the house.

Oh, the house. It was a fortress. Bars on the windows, reinforced doors, and guards patrolling the grounds. It was suffocating. The strict rules at the estate always pressed against my chest with a choking sensation when I wished for open views and fresh air. For freedom. Adventure. Not on a ship though.

As if on cue, my scar itched. Mayhap my parents felt particularly protective of me after the riding incident. But blazes, the result had been only a cut. I could have incidents anywhere—slipping on the wet cobblestones or falling down the stairs. Why would a single incident cause my parents to become so worried about my safety?

There was another, rather depressing theory about what was happening. My parents might have chosen a husband for me without telling me anything. Rennie. They wanted me to marry him, and the whole 'cruise in the Mediterranean' affair was a poor excuse to force me to be close to him. He wasn't a titled gentleman, but it didn't mean he wasn't wealthy. Father might have decided he was a good candidate for that reason, and who knew, perhaps he was a brave soldier my father deeply respected. Well, surely my parents would have never let me go with him if they didn't respect him.

A groan escaped me. It wasn't the fact that Rennie didn't hold a title. I couldn't care less about his social status or money. But our relationship hadn't started under the best circumstances, and I didn't appreciate being forced to marry anyone. I didn't like being lied to or ordered around either. And Rennie didn't trust me enough to tell me whatever was happening between my parents and him. Yes, even my parents were lying to me, but they weren't here.

Now that I wasn't feeling sick, the low rumble of the engines sounded almost lulling. The cabin, although as big as a double bedroom, was stifling, and the air was stuffy with humidity. The closer we sailed to Portugal, the warmer the air became. So I decided to take a walk on the deck. The only good thing about being on a ship was that I had a certain degree of freedom. I could take a walk without having someone breathe down my neck.

With a bit of luck, Mr Marston would be around too. It wouldn't hurt to ask him a few more questions about Sandro. He hadn't told me where and when I was supposed to meet my prince. With an enigmatic 'Sandro will find you,' he'd closed the conversation before kissing my hand.

After I slipped into a simple dark-blue dress, easy to fasten, I left my cabin. The ship never slept. At any time of night or day, there were gas lamps lit in the corridors, people walking around, and busy attendants who were always ready to help. I walked past a couple of gentlemen whose cravats were loose over their chests as they laughed and staggered on their feet.

"Evening, madam," one of them said, waving an unsteady hand.

I sped up. Cold sweat dampened my skin as I wondered if I should return to my cabin. That was the problem with having been surrounded by guards and companions all my life. I didn't know how to deal with ruffians or what to do in dangerous situations. There had always been someone to take care of me. Or maybe I was too sensitive. My parents' fears had sunk into my mind and turned me into an easily frightened damsel.

Well, not anymore. I closed my fists and soldiered onwards. If I wanted my parents to treat me like an adult, who could make her own decisions, I had to prove I was worthy of their trust.

As I climbed the stairs to the upper deck, a tingle caused the hairs behind my neck to rise. No gust of wind troubled the air. I paused and glanced around. Aside from an attendant hurrying along the passageway, I was alone. Perhaps it was my fear, still lingering within me, that made me feel jumpy. Lord, was I such a ninny?

The salty air of the sea filled my nostrils when I stepped onto the deck. The wind blew the smoke from the stacks away from me, leaving a magnificently starry sky shining above me. I tilted my head up. Oxford didn't have so many stars. The city lights and smoke covered them.

I strolled along the deck when I caught a familiar, spicy, masculine scent wafting from behind me.

I turned, and a gasp punched out of me. "Rennie!"

He was standing a few feet from me, dark and gloomy as always. "I didn't mean to give you a fright."

I inched away from him and the warmth of his body. "What are you doing here?"

"Do you feel sick again?" Genuine concern rang in his voice.

A hint of guilt pressed against my chest. "I'm fine, thank you. The effect of the green potion seems to last a long time."

"Great." He shoved his hands into his pockets and chewed on his bottom lip.

For some odd reason, the gesture captured my gaze and started a stirring in my chest. And lower.

"Do you mind if I walk with you?" he asked.

I cocked a brow, surprised that he was asking. I expected him to simply follow me as he pleased. "Not at all."

Nodding, he stepped next to me. I resumed my promenade through chaise lounges, where people used to sunbathe during the day, and sun umbrellas. The logo of the Oriental Navigation Company—two golden stars—gleamed in the starlight. I was by no means passionate about ships, especially after having been sick for days, but the quiet deck at night had its own special magic.

"Did you enjoy dancing with Mr Marston?" Rennie asked.

The tone was casual, but I caught something underneath it. Frustration? Worry?

I lifted a shoulder, not wanting to confess that Mr Marston was a far better dancer than he was. "It was a relief to do something other than be sick and wish to die."

A low chuckle came out of him. Again, the sound ensnared my attention and held it prisoner. I blamed the fresh air and the starry sky for my silly feelings.

"You can tell me the truth. I know I'm a terrible dancer." He scrubbed the back of his neck, like an embarrassed boy. "Many ladies have complained. There is nothing you can tell me that I haven't heard before. Two left feet, dancing bear, ugly ogre." A grin stretched his lips. He had quite full lips now that I noticed them. Sculpted and nicely curved.

"Ugly ogre? That's rude and not true." I cleared my throat, realising how inappropriate my comment was. "I mean, I wouldn't say you're ugly."

"But you wouldn't say I'm handsome either," he said in a flat tone.

"Actually, I would." Confound it. I should stop talking.

"Thank you." He rubbed the back of his neck again. "I'm not light or elegant, though."

"Well." I focused on the stars. "Let's just say there's room for improvement."

"You are too kind."

No, not always.

Only the sound of our footsteps echoed on the deck. Up here, the noise of the engine couldn't be heard, replaced by the rhythmic slosh of the water against the hull. Funny, but until a few hours ago, the sound had driven me mad. Now it was soothing.

"What did Mr Marston tell you?" he asked. The note of frustration I'd heard before was ringing more clearly now.

I slanted him a glare. "Why do you ask?"

"You chatted for a while with him."

"I see." I stopped, balling a fist on my hip. "That's why you followed me and joined me on this walk. You wanted to interrogate me about Edward."

"Edward? Not Mr Marston?" He worked his jaw.

"None of your business."

"I didn't follow you. I happened to be here at the same time as you. And I'm not interrogating you." Shadows played over his harsh face, adding an ounce of severity to his features. It was amazing how he could look like a boy one moment and a hard man the next. "I'm simply curious to know what he told you."

"I don't believe you. Why should I when you lied to me?" A flare of anger heated my words.

A muscle in his neck stood out in sharp relief under his skin. "I have never lied to you. I told you there are things I can't tell you."

"Then there are things I can't tell you, either." I strode past him and headed towards my cabin.

His footfalls pounded behind me. "Monia, try to understand."

"Understand what?" I didn't bother slowing my pace

or turning towards him. Or telling him he was being inappropriate again.

His strong fingers curled around my arm with surprising gentleness. "It's not my place." His heat reached my back as he stood inches from me. "To tell things."

I faced him. Somehow, the contact with him calmed my burst of anger. "What do you mean?"

"Your parents decide what you should know. Not me." For the first time, there were worry lines on his forehead. "I have to listen to them."

"But you know why they sent me away, don't you? You know everything."

We were so close that, when he inhaled, his chest brushed against mine, sending a curious jolt through my body.

"Monia." His Adam's apple bobbed up and down as he swallowed. "Yes, I do, but please don't ask me any more questions."

"I see. It's fine if you ask me questions, though." The space—the very narrow space—between us was charged with angry energy.

"I'm doing my job," he gritted out.

"Which is?"

"Keeping you safe."

There. Sandro was in danger, and my parents were worried that my association with him would put me in danger as well, and obviously, Rennie was my bodyguard. It was another reason not to reveal what Mr Marston had told me. I didn't want to accidentally put Sandro in further danger if his enemies were hunting him. I stepped away from Rennie and fiddled with the hem of my bodice, just to have something to do. The scar on my wrist pricked, as if in warning.

"I'm trying to keep you safe," he repeated. "Will you let me protect you?" The way he asked that, with his thick eyelashes lowering over his emerald eyes, softened my resolve.

"You don't need my permission."

"I do." He frowned, his hand caressing mine for a brief moment.

I exhaled. "Very well. If you really want an answer, I'd say yes. I'd be honoured to be protected by you." I meant it. My parents had chosen him, after all.

His shoulders sagged, but he narrowed his gaze, as if he weren't convinced I was telling the truth. As an awkward silence stretched between us, we didn't move away from each other; our bodies were still close enough to touch.

I averted my gaze and slipped away from him. "I wish to go back to my cabin now." Without waiting for him to say anything, I marched towards my room.

THE EFFECT OF the green potion wore off when Portugal swept into view on a clear morning. I was torn between suffering in silence and waiting stoically until we touched land, hoping the nausea would pass, or begging Rennie for another dose.

After our argument on the deck, we hadn't talked much. But I didn't want to meet Sandro while feeling sick. Also, I had to find a way to roam Lisbon alone because Rennie was going to follow me. Yes, I'd told him I agreed to have his protection, but I was free to choose when and where I wanted to be protected, wasn't I? And he would either stop me from seeing Sandro or come with me. No, thank you. I wanted answers.

As the hilly coast of Portugal became more visible, I held my breath. The wind caressed my cheeks, carrying new scents other than the saltiness of the sea, and the air lost some of its mugginess. Passengers gathered on the deck, muttering excitedly. Tourist guides would be provided to accompany us through the city of Lisbon, and I hoped to slip away from the group of passengers. We were allowed to visit the city on our own as long as we were back on board before dark, so I wasn't breaking any rules. My bodyguard was the problem.

Rennie stood next to me, his face a map of hard lines of worry. Despite the warm weather, he was wearing his grey suit, identical to the one my father wore to work.

I fiddled with my reticule and turned to him. "I don't feel very well."

He whipped his head towards me. "Do you prefer staying in your cabin? I don't mind staying with you if you want." Maybe it was my imagination, but there was a note of hope in his voice. "I can fetch you some tea and a book. Or ask the physician on board to have a look at you."

If I agreed, he'd watch my every move. I had more

chances of losing him in Lisbon. Although, his plan didn't sound so terrible. A cup of tea and a good book. "No, I want to visit the city. I'd like some green potion if you still have it."

"Of course." He took out a vial from his breast pocket and handed it to me. "Only a small sip."

"I know."

The moment the green potion hit my tongue, my nausea vanished. Excitement flared up at the chance to see Sandro again and to have some answers. Energy rushed through my veins with a healthy dose of optimism. My sense of adventure grabbed me by the throat, chasing away my fears and insecurities. Yes, I could sneak away unnoticed and wander in a city I'd never been to before, filled with people who spoke a language I didn't know, without getting lost, robbed, or killed. All to find an elusive prince, whom I wasn't even sure was in Lisbon and who was potentially dangerous. Cup of tea. No more fear. I was a new woman. Yes, I was.

I searched the crowd of passengers for Mr Marston, but there were too many people. Rennie's scrutiny was as thick as a blanket, but I did my best to ignore it. He could keep his secrets. I had mine.

"Better?" he asked.

I nodded, handing him the vial. I returned my attention to the sea while he stood next to me, stiff and serious. "Do you ever have a moment to rest and enjoy yourself?" I asked him, curious.

"Of course I do."

"What do you like to do when you aren't working?" I enjoyed the fact that, when asked questions that didn't pertain to my parents, he answered them.

"I like sparring."

"No? You? I would've never guessed," I quipped, propping an elbow on the handrail.

He barked a throaty laugh. "And if I tell you I like whittling, would you be surprised?"

"Yes?"

"Look." From his pocket, he fished out a few-inch-long wooden squirrel. Half of its body was still a piece of rough wood, but the details of the nose, bushy tail, and eyes were exquisite. It was hard to imagine his big hands capable of producing something so delicate and small.

"It's beautiful. My word, you're talented."

He swallowed and put a hand on the back of his neck, his cheeks flushing. "Well, yes, thank you." He pocketed the squirrel and avoided my gaze.

"Where did you learn?"

"At school. A boarding school." His voice sounded distant and detached.

"It doesn't seem like you were happy there." I must have said something wrong because he pressed his lips together, every trace of the shy boy gone.

"We've nearly arrived," he said, pointing at the land.

Fine. I didn't press him. His past wasn't a secret I wanted him to reveal to me unless he volunteered the information. So I waited.

We hadn't nearly arrived.

It took the SS *Florentia* two hours to enter the port, and then another good hour passed before the attendants told us we could disembark.

"Do you want to follow the guide?" Rennie asked as we walked along the gangplank.

"Er, of course. It would be lovely." I faked a smile.

"Perfect."

A string of horse-pulled wagons waited for us on the platform. I climbed into one, followed by a brooding Rennie, and we drove towards the city. My mouth dropped open at the sight of the River Tagus. It must be ten times the width of the Thames because the opposite shore wasn't visible. Cathedrals and colourful houses with red, green, and yellow walls streamed past us, casting their shadows on the cobbled street. Then Belém Tower swept into view, tall and majestic with its white and yellow stone bricks, and I forgot about my rendezvous. Even Rennie was watching the city, his scowl gone for once as he leant closer to the window.

"Is it the first time you've seen Lisbon?" I asked, genuinely curious.

He grinned, a smile that made me smile. "I haven't travelled much. I've been to Paris once, for work, but aside from that, I've never left British soil." There was something boyish and sad in the way he said it. My chest clenched a little for him.

"I'm glad looking after me is bringing you some joy," I said. "At least this job gives you something new."

And just like that, the scowl was back, but he didn't say

anything. He withdrew to a corner of the seat, brooding. Oh, well. I wouldn't let his dark mood ruin mine. I was about to see Sandro again.

The road became steep. I grabbed hold of a rail as the wagon jolted. The caravan of wagons was crawling up a hill. Ugh. Their swinging and rocking were similar to those of the sea, and I sat back on my seat. My knees touched Rennie's when the wagon lurched again. Immediate heat spilt into my cheeks as my body reminded me of his gentle fingers on my naked back. He shifted on his seat and inched away from me. After a few turns and more jolts, the wagon slowed. When we stepped out of it, the hot, dry air enveloped my body. Instead, Rennie seemed at ease in his suit.

The guide, dressed in a blue uniform with the symbol of the two stars on his chest, gestured towards the castle looming over us. Tall, thick walls, towers, and turrets partially obscured the sun.

"Gather around, passengers from the SS *Florentia*," the man said.

Feet shuffled and excited mutters spread.

The guide smiled. "St Jorge Castle was built during the Moorish occupation of Portugal..."

Distracted by Mr Marston, I didn't hear the rest of the story. He was standing on the other side of the group, half-hidden behind a broad man. His hair caught the sunlight as he turned towards me. He touched the tip of his hat and bowed his head. I returned the greeting with a quick nod. Then he pointed a finger at the castle, wiggling his eyebrows before nodding again. So Sandro was there. My mouth grew dry. I forced my face to remain deadpan while my pulse sped up. My legs trembled when we started to walk along the stone bridge that led to the entrance. Rennie's shoulder touched mine, and I jolted.

"Are you all right?" he asked, peering at me.

"Spectacular, thank you."

He shot me a narrowed gaze.

I breathed harder when we climbed a stone staircase and finally stopped in a yard next to the statue of a lion. Rusty cannons were pointing towards the sea, and Rennie strode towards one—the least interesting feature of the castle, in my opinion. Who would look at a rusted metal piece when there was a magnificent stone lion? Anyway, he forgot about me. Good. Although the way he watched the cannon, muttering under his breath, made me wonder if he'd stare at a woman he liked in the same fashion. On second thought, who cared? Not me.

"Part of the castle is in ruins, due to an earthquake that struck the city in the eighteenth century," the guide said.

But even damaged, the castle radiated power and strength. The view was stunning. The blue of the ocean mixed with the different colours of the city and—"Monia," a velvety male voice whispered close to me.

I turned towards the voice. It was Mr Marston. "Edward, I mean, Mr Marston."

He flashed a charming smirk. "Call me Edward, please."

I glanced at Rennie, who was still gaping at the

cannon, hands on his hips and mouth open as if he hadn't seen anything more beautiful.

"I will," I said.

Edward pointed a discreet finger to his left. "Follow that passageway and turn right. Sandro is waiting for you there."

"Sandro is—thank you!" I squeezed his hand on impulse and, after checking that Rennie was still engrossed by the dull cannon, I scurried away. Escaping had been easier than I'd thought.

My heels clicked on the white stones as I half-ran, half-walked towards the end of the passageway. When I turned right and found myself in another cosy yard, Sandro's name left my lips in a whisper. For a brief moment, I caught a glimpse of a tall, dark-haired man watching me from underneath the portico. Eyes the colour of midnight lured me in. I ran towards him, my feet barely touching the ground. "Sandro!"

But the image must have been a trick of the sunlight and my imagination because, when I blinked, he was gone. I skidded to a stop. Wisps of my hair escaped my bun and were brushing against my cheeks. I rushed from one corner of the yard to another, checking the stone columns that enclosed it, but no one was there.

"Sandro?" I called.

Only the breeze answered. I stomped a foot on the ground. Tarnation. I was sure I'd seen him.

"Monia!" Rennie's deep voice thundered in the yard. His heavy footsteps were beating at an angry tempo.

Wheezing, I leant my back against the cool wall and silently cursed him.

Oh, he was furious, if the hard slant of his mouth and the ice in his gaze were any indication. But the crushing disappointment souring my mouth was too strong for me to care about his mood.

"Why did you leave the group?" He took my shoulders with gentle hands, a muscle ticking in his jaw. "What are you doing here?" Fear sneaked into his words.

"Can't I have a moment for myself? I'm a tourist. I was... touring." Blazes, I'd never been a good liar, but at that moment, I sounded on the verge of madness.

"What were you doing here?" The tone of his voice dropped dangerously. The fear was gone, replaced by suspicion. His delicate touch on my shoulders was a stark contrast to the harshness in his question.

"You don't answer any of my questions. I don't see why I should answer yours." I tried to shrug free, but he held me in place.

His grip wasn't painful, but it was firm enough to make me feel the strength of his fingers. "Monia, this is serious. Tell me the truth." He sounded concerned now, but I didn't care.

"Sorry, but I can't." Throwing back his words at him, I shrugged free from his grip.

"Monia," he hissed, but I didn't bother answering.

I rushed away from him, angry tears burning my eyes.

FOUR

AFTER A DAY spent under the implacable Portuguese sun and walking up and down hills, I was almost glad to crawl back to the dark and cool SS *Florentia*. I wasn't glad to face three more days at sea before we stopped in Tunis. I was much less glad to face Rennie, who'd been following me everywhere like a hunter, since my failed escape.

I dragged myself towards my cabin, looking forward to washing away the dust of the day and changing into something lighter. The disappointment at not having seen Sandro was like a thorn in my chest. No Sandro, no answers. Rennie tailed me along the cool passageway, radiating annoyance and clenching his fists.

A scoff left me when I put my hand on the doorknob. "Are you going to follow me everywhere now?"

He folded his muscular arms over his chest. "You've proven to be untrustworthy even though you agreed to let me do my job and protect you."

"I'm not a child."

"Then don't behave like one."

"Confound it." I pushed the door open and slammed it shut behind him. Not very mature. I was only confirming his words. But his constant presence was itching along my skin, and today's fisco didn't help my mood.

I washed and changed, taking my time brushing my hair and choosing a dress for dinner. Unfortunately, every evening dress in my trunk had buttons on the back. When I'd packed my clothes, I'd been in a hurry, thanks to my parents. But I'd rather show my naked back to every passenger than ask Rennie for help. Bother. The dress was a tad large for my straight body. If I breathed too hard, it might slip down. Never mind. I'd be careful.

So I wrapped myself in my shawl, leaving my back half-naked underneath. When I opened the door, I wasn't surprised to find Rennie in the corridor.

His jacket hung from the rail. His shirtsleeves were rolled up to his elbows, showing his corded muscles, and the waistcoat stretched over his chest. The yellow glow from the gas lamps enhanced the scar on his neck and the harsh set of his jaw. He looked every inch the pugilist, which I was sure he was.

"Are you ready to go to dinner?" he asked between clenched teeth.

"Yes." I straightened and turned towards the other side of the passageway.

There was a low rumble, coming from somewhere, as if

the engine were hiccupping. The floor shook. I gasped and grabbed the rail, my stomach lurching. Rennie's hand took my elbow.

"Stormy weather," he said, steadying me.

"Indeed." I snatched my arm free and started walking again.

The muscles in his naked arms, contracting and tensing, were quite distracting. Not that I was staring. Why would I care? But I hadn't seen many half-naked men in my life, and he was displaying lots of muscles. Gentlemen didn't show their arms, especially at dinner.

"Shouldn't you wear your jacket for dinner?" I asked, eyeing him again.

"Shouldn't you have your dress fully buttoned for dinner?"

Annoyance tickled me as my mouth hung open. "Listen—" My little speech was cut off by another jolt from the ship. I lost my balance and fell back. Rennie caught me and pulled me closer to his hard body.

As he went to withdraw his arm, my dress caught in the newel cap with a yank. The noise of ripped fabric boomed in the silent passageway. Pearly buttons rained to the floor and ended up under my slippers, causing me to lose my balance again. It was like ice skating. Not that I'd done that often. Safety and all that. Too dangerous for me, according to my parents.

"Confound it." I had to grip Rennie's shoulders not to fall over.

The back of my dress unfastened completely, and the low neckline dropped a few inches, revealing the top of my breasts and the lacy hem of my chemise. If I tilted my head to the right angle, I could see my nipples, taut and pressed against the flimsy fabric, which meant that Rennie could see them too.

His lips parted in mute shock as his gaze dipped low, down to my neckline, and stayed there. He was so focused on the show I was accidentally offering that he didn't even blink. My cheeks flamed. And not only them. The heat moved lower, much lower. A combination of shame and something else I didn't want to acknowledge caused me to freeze in his arms.

Then the SS *Florentia* jolted again, shoving me into Rennie's arms. My half-naked breasts rubbed against his chest. The dress dipped another inch, revealing my nipples. He kept staring with undisguised interest. Another shock of stillness went through me as the contact with his broad body started an illicit pulse between my thighs.

Holy. Smoke.

Unless I untangled myself from his embrace, we would stay here and... and... I didn't want to think about *that*. With the speed of a startled mouse, I scurried away from him and covered my chest with my shawl.

"I need to change," I stuttered the most obvious words I'd ever spoken.

Without waiting for him to say anything, I ran towards my cabin. Of course, he hounded me. His footfalls echoed in the passageway. When I tried to open the door, the key to my cabin slid out of my fingers and clattered to the floor, thanks to my trembling fingers. Before I could pick it up, Rennie took it for me and unlocked the door.

"Monia, I should apologise," he said in a low, intense voice that started a stirring in my belly, but I didn't want to hear anything.

I brushed past him and slipped inside my cabin, gazing at the floor. Stubbornly, he followed me inside and shut the door. I was alone with him!

"Monia, I..." He scrubbed the back of his neck, shoulders hunched.

"We're alone in my cabin." Sheer shock and outrage caused my voice to quiver. "You should leave."

"Yes, sorry. Of course." He opened the door, then closed it. "It's that... I... All right. I'll leave you alone." In a flutter of grey fabric, he staggered out of the cabin, leaving behind a heady male scent.

Blimey. My shoulders sagged when I was finally alone. That had been embarrassing. No. If I was being honest with myself, it'd been exciting, too. A little. Watching him lose his cold composure because he was staring at me had been empowering, different, and adventurous.

I shook my head, discarding the shawl and the half-ripped dress. Forget fashion. I was going to wear a dress I could button on my own. The SS *Florentia* rocked gently, as if in agreement, before giving a lurch.

"Dash it all." I gripped the table to steady myself. And they said big ships didn't rock around.

After I changed into a blue afternoon dress that buttoned on the front, I was surprised not to see Rennie waiting for me in the passageway. I must have scared him away. I was alone. Good. Yes, it was good. Freedom at last. What I wanted, right?

After glancing right and left to be sure he wasn't lurking somewhere, I strode towards the reception area. The ship inclined again with a violent jolt, and I was thrown against the wall. Pain exploded in my shoulder after the impact. Thank goodness nausea wasn't a problem for now. Wincing, I rubbed the sore spot and resumed walking. A young woman stood behind the reception desk, struggling to stand up while keeping the ink bottle straight. Since Rennie wasn't tailing me, I should take advantage of the rare moment of freedom to do some investigation.

"This is perfectly normal, madam," she said before I asked her anything. "The captain said we're leaving behind the rogue waves. In a few minutes, everything will be fine."

"That's great, but I meant to ask you something else." As I straightened, so did the ship.

The chandeliers hanging from the ceiling jingled when the crystals hit each other, casting shimmering lights on the white walls.

"How can I help you?" she asked.

I searched around again. Rennie could be awfully silent. "I'm looking for a passenger, Mr Edward Marston. I'd like to know the number of his cabin."

"Let me see." She brushed her dishevelled locks from her face and flipped through the pages of a register. Her brow furrowed. "Are you sure the gentleman's name is correct? I can't find any Marston."

"I'm sure. I met him at dinner."

"Maybe he isn't a passenger but a member of the staff." She opened another register and went through it.

A pricking started at the base of my neck. Edward wasn't part of the crew. He didn't wear a uniform.

She shook her head. "No, madam. I'm sorry. There is no Edward Marston on board."

"But I talked to him. I danced with him."

Sighing, she put the registers aside. "Then perhaps there was a misunderstanding about his name. Maybe the gentleman has a longer name, and he gave you his middle name."

Or he'd lied to me. Dash it. I didn't know what to believe. "Thank you."

Why would Edward lie? Was he implicated in Sandro's problems? Was he a spy? What advantage would he get from lying to me?

I returned to my cabin to see if Rennie was waiting for me there. But no. The corridor was empty. Odd. I loitered, torn between going to dinner and enjoying an evening alone, or going to his cabin and checking on him. But he could take care of himself, and Edward might be in the dining hall. Without Rennie breathing down my neck, I would have time to talk with Edward undisturbed. I spun on my heels and started heading for the dining hall, only to come to an abrupt stop. I chewed on my bottom lip, doubt gnawing at me. What if Rennie had fallen and hurt himself? There had been a few mighty jolts, and he hadn't been himself when he'd left my cabin. The fact he wasn't here bothered me more than I wanted to admit. I sighed.

Fine. I would go and see him.

The ship slanted right and left, but not with the same wild energy as before. I could walk along the passageway without tripping on my feet. Rennie's cabin was on the lower floor, second class. My cabin was suffocating, but I had a clear view of the sea and sky. I guessed Rennie's cabin must be even more oppressive.

The polished wooden floor and the golden decorations that abounded in first class were replaced by ugly brown tiles and dull wallpaper in second class. The corridor was narrower than the one upstairs, and the lights were few and far between. Even the floorboards were uneven.

I knocked on door number seventeen. "Rennie?" A muffled noise, like a strangled moan, came from the other side of the door. "Rennie? Are you all right?"

Another groan.

"I'm coming in." Pulse spiking, I turned the knob and inched the door inward. "Are you—"

From a corner of the dimly lit cabin, a huge man emerged and shoved me back with enough strength to make me lose my balance. I had barely time to let out a scream before I fell over and hit the floor hard. A new pang shot up my shoulders. The man scampered out of the room, hitting my stomach with a kick in the process. The groan of pain I meant to release remained trapped in my chest as I curled up into a ball, pain bursting through me.

Agony radiated from my belly to my brain, a burning sensation that punched the breath out of my lungs. Even my head spun.

"Monia." Rennie's rough voice came from somewhere in the cabin.

There was a noise of feet shuffling across the floor. Then his warm hand was on my shoulder.

"Did he hurt you?" Lord, his voice sounded wrong, all raspy and broken, as if he were about to cry. What had happened to him?

Gasping, I opened my mouth. "F-fine."

He stroked my cheek with so much kindness that I leant against his touch. "Let me turn on a lamp." More groans of pain rose from him.

He limped around and rummaged through the room lit by the light from the corridor. A yellow glow spread from the nightstand, illuminating the chaos in the cabin. Shards of glass littered the floor. The bed sheets had been ripped, and Rennie's clothes were scattered around.

As the pain in my belly faded, I sat upright, my body shivering. "What happened? Who was that man?"

"I don't know." He limped back towards me and crouched.

The light revealed all the red spots marring his face and a deep gash in his side where a wet dark patch stained his waistcoat.

"Rennie." On pure instinct, I put a hand on his cheek, feeling the light stubble. "Did he stab you?"

"I'm fine."

Maybe I was too shocked by what had happened, but I could swear he leant against my touch as well.

"You aren't fine. You must go to see the doctor immediately." I stroked his cheek. His skin was surprisingly smooth.

"I don't need a doctor. Don't worry." He held my hand, his breathing returning to normal.

"Don't worry?" I stood up on wobbly legs. He staggered to his feet too, wincing all the way up. "You aren't fine at all. Let's go." I slid an arm around his waist and dragged him towards the door. Or tried to. He didn't budge. "Rennie." I squeezed him harder. "You're injured."

A softness relaxed his features, which didn't make any sense. He'd been attacked. "I don't need a doctor. Trust me."

"You're bleeding. Why do you have to be so stubborn? We must report the attack to the security officer. For Pete's sake."

He put a hand over mine and sucked in a deep breath. A battle was raging inside him, judging by the way his lips were pressed together and the worry lines creased his forehead.

"All right," he gritted out, as if reluctant to accept the evidence that he was bleeding and needed medical attention. Rennie and his stupid stubbornness.

We inched out of the room with Rennie's heavy body nearly dragging me down.

"What happened?" I asked as we slogged towards the stairs.

He swallowed hard. "I entered my cabin and shut the door. The next moment, the man jumped out of a corner and attacked me. Then you came."

"And your leg?"

Another grimace twisted his mouth. "The man nearly broke it with a kick. He's strong."

A sickening lump of anxiety swelled in my throat. "Good Lord, Rennie. The gush? Is it a stab?"

"I think so. It was too dark to see his blade, though," he said as if he were talking about a stroll in the park.

A few passengers glanced at us when we reached the main deck. Whispers and mutters followed us.

"I don't understand." I shook my head, Rennie's arm weighing me down. "What did he want? If he wanted money, he should have broken into a first-class cabin. I mean no offence by that."

A smirk tugged at his lips. "None taken."

"Why was he attacking you? Did you anger him?"

Rennie paused, his eyebrows drawing together. "Where does this idea come from? I don't even know the man."

"Well, you know. It's a logical conclusion." I shrugged. "Perhaps he said something, you said something, and he attacked you."

Scoffing, he resumed slogging forwards. "Logical conclusion my arse," he muttered.

I paused. "Manners!"

His reply was a groan. What an impossible man.

"I'm sorry," he whispered.

"Never mind. You've been stabbed." I waved dismissively.

"No, I mean, I'm sorry for having stared." He avoided gazing at me.

"Oh." I staggered under his weight, and he held me upright. "Don't worry. We have more pressing matters at the moment."

"Yes, but my behaviour was inexcusable." He shook his head.

"Let's forget about the whole incident, shall we?" Because I was going to be the first woman to die of embarrassment.

He grimaced. "Damn, it hurts."

The smell of carbolic acid filled the air when we made our way along a pristine white passageway. We stopped in front of a set of double doors with the name of a doctor written on a plaque. There was no one in the passageway, and the room behind the doors was empty. Great.

"Hmm, help?" I shouted. What did a bleeding passenger have to do to get medical attention?

Finally, a couple of nurses came out of the lateral doors.

Twenty minutes later, a nurse was visiting me while a doctor was attending to Rennie's wounds in another room. She was the same red-haired girl I'd seen when I'd been dancing with Edward.

"Good gracious, madam," she said, applying an ointment to the huge black bruise on my ribs. Her gaze flickered over the scar on my arm, but she didn't comment.

"That deranged man kicked you so very hard. You're lucky he didn't break any ribs."

"It felt like he did." I winced as she probed around the bruise. "Every time I inhale, it hurts."

"I'm sorry. I'm sure the security officers will catch the man soon."

I released a breath when she finished attending to the bruise. "I remember having seen you in the dancing hall the other night. You said my partner and I were good dancers."

"Of course, I remember you, madam." She smiled, wiping her hands on a towel.

"Do you know Edward, the man I was dancing with? It seems he can't be found anywhere on the ship. I asked the lady at the reception desk, but she couldn't find his name on any lists."

"That's surprising." A little frown creased her forehead. "But surely, other people must have noticed him. He was so handsome. His long black hair and sharp grey eyes aren't common."

Black hair? Grey eyes? I stopped buttoning my dress. "I think there's a misunderstanding. Edward has blond hair and blue eyes."

Her frown deepened. "I'm sure the man I saw you with had long black hair tied in a bun at the base of his neck and grey eyes, madam."

The description didn't fit Edward at all. "We're talking about two different men. I didn't dance with any man with long dark hair." I couldn't completely remove the frustration from my voice. But honestly. She remembered me, but not Edward. Was she making fun of me?

There was a moment of awkward silence. The nurse stared at me, as if wondering if she should check my head as well. The knock on the door broke the spell.

"May I come in?" a man said from the other side.

I tugged at my shirt and patted my hair. "You may."

A man in a dark blue uniform with the golden stars of the company bowed to me from the threshold. His rounded glasses perched on his straight nose. "Miss Fitzwilliam, I'm Detective Norton. I'm terribly sorry for the incident. I promise I will start a thorough investigation and catch the perpetrator as soon as possible." He flipped through the pages of a notepad. "Would you please tell me what happened?"

I didn't have much to say. It took me only a couple of minutes to sum up how the huge man had tackled me and kicked me in the stomach before rushing out of Rennie's cabin. Pain burned my side all over again as I remembered the kick. My breathing sped up.

Norton nodded. "Can you describe the man?"

"It was dark, but I can tell you he was tall, muscular, and broad."

The detective stopped writing, scowling. "Are you sure, madam?"

"As I said, it was dark. I'm not sure about the colour of the man's hair or eyes, but I'm pretty sure he was a large, strong man."

Norton scribbled something in the notepad, shooting

me a glare, as if I were a lunatic. He exchanged a glance with the nurse. "Large and strong?" he repeated.

Hadn't I been clear enough? "Yes," I said.

He wrote something else. "That's all for now. Thank you, madam."

FIVE

CLEANED FROM THE blood and with a bandage around his hand, Rennie was waiting for me in the passageway after I left the medical centre. He roamed his gaze over me, but it wasn't the heated glance he'd given me when my dress had fallen apart. It was a clinical, searching-for-injuries look.

"Are you all right?" he asked, sounding sweetly concerned for me.

"Only a bruise." I patted my ribs. "How are you?"

He stretched out a hand, as if to squeeze my shoulder, but then he withdrew it. "I stink of carbolic acid."

I took a sniff. He was right. His heady scent had been replaced with the acrid smell of coal tar and the Burnett's liquid physicians used to clean wounds.

"I prefer your clean scent," I said before I could stop my stupid mouth.

His lips parted. "Do you?"

"Oh, well..." I coughed into my closed fist. "Let's retire. I'm rather tired." I didn't miss the satisfied grin pulling up a corner of his mouth.

In silence, we dragged ourselves towards our cabins. The ship had stopped rocking, and an eerie quietness filled the passageways.

"Do you think Detective Norton will catch the man?" I asked as we approached my cabin.

He shrugged. "It shouldn't be difficult. It's a bloody ship."

I rolled my eyes at his rudeness. I was about to tell him that Edward had seemingly disappeared and the nurse was ridiculously confused about his features, but I thought better of it. He would ask questions and pry around, and I didn't want him to find out the connection between Edward and Sandro.

When we stopped in front of my cabin, I faced him, a hand on my bruise. "Good night, then. And please go to the doctor if you feel sick."

He loitered, scratching his chin and studying me with his keen gaze. "Lock yourself in and put a chair against the door. Don't let anyone in except me. Understood?"

I wasn't going to argue with him. I doubted the man would attack me, but the pain in my ribs was a good reminder that anything could happen. "Understood."

"Good night." Without adding anything else, he staggered away.

"Rennie!" I called, gripping my door.

He stopped and turned to me. "Yes?" His large green eyes widened. Lord, they were pretty.

Why had I called him? I had no idea. It'd been a moment of irrational fear as he left me alone. Blazes, what was I thinking? Being alone was what I wanted, wasn't it?

"Yes?" he asked more gently, stepping closer. For once, the harshness was gone from his eyes. Only concern shone in their depths.

"I don't know," I whispered. "I don't know why I called you. Sorry."

He lifted a hand and traced the curve of my jaw with a silky touch that made my knees weak. "Are you scared?"

"A bit, to be honest."

"Would you like me to stand guard here?"

"Good Lord, no." I frowned. "You need to sleep. I got bruised, but you got stabbed. I'll be all right." Actually, a tremor started in my legs, but I shifted my weight. I was used to having someone close at all times. In my parents' mansion, a maid slept in the room next to mine. I wanted my freedom, but Hades if I wasn't scared. Yet I wouldn't let him neglect his own health for me.

His thumb brushed my jaw, sending a warm flutter down my spine. "If you need anything, you only have to call. Don't worry about waking me up."

I nodded as a sudden knot blocked my throat.

"Good night, Monia." He withdrew his hand and limped away, leaving me somewhat colder than before.

BRIGHT SUNLIGHT FLOODED my cabin the next morning. I brushed my matted hair from my face after a rough night's sleep. Fatigue had won over my fears, allowing me to sleep. But nightmares had tormented me. Sharp teeth, a burning pain in my arm, and a strange creature. Visions of blood soaking my riding habit and the sensation of being stabbed in the arm had jolted me awake a few times. I rubbed my aching forehead, glad the sunlight made the cabin look bigger. Sweat soaked my nightgown, and I scoffed while cleaning myself up.

I smiled when I opened the door and found Rennie waiting for me in the corridor. "How are you? You should be resting."

"Don't worry." He shrugged. "I've been better, but I've seen worse. Your bruise?"

"Painful, but better than last night." I tilted my head, noticing he kept his posture straight. "How's your wound?"

"It wasn't as deep as you thought. Barely a scratch."

"It bled a lot." I wasn't an expert in wounds, but his stab had been serious.

"I'm starving. Shall we go to the dining hall?"

"Of course." Odd.

He walked next to me, shooting glares at anyone who brushed past us. His shoulders were stiff and tense.

I put a hand on his arm. "Don't be so tense. He won't attack us in broad daylight."

His gaze dipped to my hand before returning to my face. But he didn't say anything.

Having skipped supper last night, my stomach

rumbled in appreciation as I scooped up spoons full of porridge.

Rennie sat next to me, barely touching his scrambled eggs, his gaze lost on the sea.

"I thought you were hungry. Are you thinking about the man from last night?" I asked, polishing my bowl.

He leant back, drumming his fingers on the table. "I don't understand how he entered my cabin. I opened the door with my key. The door was locked and wasn't broken, so he didn't force it. He either picked the lock or had a master key. Odd."

"Both explanations are reasonable. A professional thief should know how to pick the lock of a cabin, and he could have stolen a master key from a member of the crew. Why don't you find those two explanations valid?" I poured myself another cup of tea, studying Rennie's profile.

His rough charm started a flutter in my chest. Sandro was handsome with his fine features, but I could see the appeal of a wilder, rougher appearance. No bruise marred Rennie's skin. I thought the man had punched him. He had to be a fast healer. Very fast.

"I don't know. It's just a feeling I have." The sunlight lit his eyes, turning them into two emeralds. His cheeks were pale though. "Listen." He lifted his gaze to me. "Why don't we go back to England? Now. Leave this bloody ship and return home."

"What?" I lowered my cup, nearly spilling the tea. "What are you talking about? I've just started to enjoy myself now that I don't feel sick every two minutes, and you want to leave? Besides, the trip would be a rather uncomfortable one. We'd either travel by train, stopping countless times across countries with names I can't even pronounce and spending weeks in a carriage, or take another ship, and what would the difference be then? Not to mention that we need to stop in Tunis anyway."

He chewed his bottom lip, and for some stupid reason, my eyes focused on the way the tip of his tongue appeared from between his white teeth. He had nice white teeth, I guessed.

"You're right. Forget it." Rennie waved a dismissive hand. But I wasn't fooled.

"Why are you so worried?" I asked. His hand lay a few inches from mine, and I stifled the odd urge to brush it. The truth was he radiated sadness and fear, and my chest tightened for him. "I understand the whole ordeal must have traumatised you, but we can't let that thug scare us, can we?"

"I'm not *traumatised*." His usual scowl was back, erasing his moment of weakness. "I'm worried about your safety. Obviously, this ship has her share of criminals. You aren't safe. I don't like it."

I took another sip of tea, spying on him from over the rim of my cup. "Are you worried about me, or are you overzealous about doing your duty?"

His emerald eyes, which I'd admired so much, turned into two stormy pits. "Now you're being unfair. Of course, I'm worried about you. Sod the work. This is about your safety." His voice cracked when he said the last words.

I blew out a breath. "I think you're overreacting. At the end of the day, nothing really happened, and Detective Norton—"

"Help!" A woman barged into the dining hall, her grey-striped hair bouncing over her reddened cheeks.

I was on my feet before I knew it. Rennie was faster than me, though. Attendants and other passengers rushed to her aid.

"What is it, madam?" I took her trembling shoulders. "Are you hurt?"

"A man attacked me." Her voice was so high-pitched it could cut glass. Gasps echoed in the room. "I was coming here to have breakfast when he emerged from a dark corner and jumped on me." She clamped her hands over her rising bosom.

"Here, sit down." I gently led her to my chair and helped her sit, ignoring the whispers and mutters from the crowd. "What is your name, madam?"

She swallowed a couple of times. "Mrs Agnes Francis."

"You're safe now, Mrs Francis." I patted her shoulder. "Here, have a cup of tea."

"Call the doctor," Rennie barked at the attendants who were standing close, gaping at us.

A few people darted out of the hall, and the attendants dispersed the crowd.

"Can you describe him?" Rennie asked Mrs Francis in a gentle tone.

She patted her dishevelled curls. "Oh, he was a strapping young man with curly red hair and lovely blue eyes.

Straight nose. Strong jaw." As she talked, her breathing slowed and she stopped fiddling with her hands. "Quite handsome. And he was wearing a beautiful kilt that left his legs bare. Strong, muscular legs, that is. Broad shoulders and strong arms, too. When he swept me off my feet into his embrace, like a knight of old helping the damsel..." She coughed, her cheeks flushing further. "Well, he was strapping and handsome. That's all."

I exchanged a glance with Rennie. Mrs Francis didn't seem terrified by the attack but rather excited by the encounter.

Rennie bowed to her. "Madam, I'll have a look around and inform the police on board. Please stay here."

"Thank you." She put a hand on his and smiled.

While Rennie made his way across the hall packed with whispering passengers, she tilted her head to stare at his rear. Good Lord. Was she admiring Rennie's bottom? After being attacked? Although I couldn't blame her. Rennie could be scary, but his rear end wasn't bad at all. All firm and taut, stretching the fabric of his trousers. Naked, he must be a sight to behold. Dear me. What a thought to have. Mrs Francis's excitement had to be contagious.

"You must be quite upset," I said to distract myself from my inappropriate thoughts.

"Oh, it was exciting as well." She winked.

I was confused. "Exciting?"

"He kissed me, and good gracious, it was such a passionate kiss."

I was even more confused. "I'm sorry, madam, but did he force you?"

She gazed around, ignoring my question.

"Here I am." The red-haired nurse hurried towards Mrs Francis. "Please come with me, madam. I'll take good care of you." She narrowed her gaze at me, probably still annoyed by our conversation.

"Thank you, dear," Mrs Francis said, walking away.

I stayed in the dining hall, enjoying another cup of tea while waiting for Rennie. Wasn't that odd? Two attacks, one after another, from two different men, although I doubted Mrs Francis was as distraught as I'd been after the man had kicked me.

Rennie walked over to me, his face tense and the tendons in his neck standing out under his skin.

"Is something the matter?" I asked, lowering my cup.

Worry lines marked his brow as he sat next to me. "I couldn't find any trace of a Scotsman. Among the passengers, there are only five Scots, and none of them fit the description of Mrs Francis's attacker."

"Anyone can wear a kilt." My voice lacked confidence, though. There was something plainly bizarre about the attack.

"Yes, but who would be so foolish to attack a woman in broad daylight, on a ship, surrounded by other people a few yards away while wearing a rather noticeable kilt? I can't find any—" He fell silent and ran a hand over his face. "Hellfire."

"You can't find what?" I edged closer.

"Nothing," he muttered.

"Rennie." I couldn't help it and put my hand on his, stroking the rough skin over his knuckles. I wasn't prepared for the shock of sensation coursing through me as he stared at me with an intensity that made me gasp. "What is it? You can trust me. I'll help you. I'll do my best."

"I know you'll help me." His thumb caressed my fingers. "And I trust you."

A warm flutter started in my chest and went lower, heating my body all the way down. I explored his hand, touching the tiny scars and calluses. I wanted to ask him how he got the scar on his neck, but speaking would break the moment, and I didn't want to stop touching him.

We stared into each other's eyes. I didn't know what was happening to us and didn't care. Then he gently turned my hand, so that my palm faced up, and dipped his head. A breath tore out of me as he placed a soft kiss on my inner wrist. My mouth dropped open. The kiss was gentle, yet passionate, and the soft scratching of his stubble against my hand fired energy through me. A tingle burned my skin, and the flutter deep in my belly became a storm of emotion. His soft lips brushed another kiss that made me catch my breath. He paused, his gaze on the inch of scarred skin peeping from underneath the hem of my sleeve.

"An incident," I whispered.

He kissed the scarred spot before stroking it with his thumb. Each stroke sent a shot of pleasure through my body. Too much pleasure. I didn't expect that.

He released my hand. "I apologise. I don't claim to be a gentleman, but my behaviour is inexcusable."

"I beg to differ." I couldn't lie. I enjoyed his touch.

His lips parted in surprise. "Are you sure?"

"Very." I caressed his fingers, listening to his breathing speed up.

He swallowed hard. "This shouldn't... I think I need to go."

I didn't have time to add anything else before he scraped his chair back and rose. With long strides, he crossed the dining hall and disappeared. My skin prickled where he'd kissed me. I didn't know what was more mysterious—the attacks or Rennie.

THE MOST EXCITING thing that happened in the next two days was seeing the Rock of Gibraltar as the *SS Florentia* officially entered the Mediterranean Sea.

The rocky white peak rose from the sea like a giant fang, a stark contrast to the turquoise waves. Rennie had been more taciturn than usual since our brief kiss, leaving me confused. I'd told him I enjoyed his touch. Why then was he so cold?

Even now that we were both on the main deck, admiring the view, he remained silent, hands in his pockets, glowering. Every time I caught a glimpse of his lips, the spot on my wrist he'd kissed tickled. But he hadn't talked much in the past two days and had touched me even less. Which was a pity. Not that I craved his touch. No, sir. All I had to do was ignore the sudden lurch of my heart when he was close to me, the traitorous quiver of my knees when our gazes met, or the heat flooding my cheeks when he rolled his bottom lip between his teeth. Cup of tea, really.

For example, he moved closer and his elbow brushed mine. A sudden shot of excitement jolted through me and made me tingle in all the wrong places. But I controlled it. I wasn't a woman prone to swooning over a gentleman. Sandro had made me swoon a little. But to be honest, Sandro's touch hadn't been so raw and exciting. Pleasant, yes. Charming, of course. But not soul-wrenching like Rennie's. I cleared my throat and let the wind cool my warm cheeks. Maybe I was craving his touch.

"No news on the thugs roaming the ship?" I asked when the ship left Gibraltar behind.

"Nothing. Detective Norton searched every cabin but couldn't find a man who matched the description I gave him or who matched Mrs Francis's attacker." He shook his head. "How hard can it be to find a young, bald man with a missing finger?"

"What?" I spun towards him, a hand on my straw hat. What bald man?

"Mr Steele?" The detective in question approached us. He flashed a nervous smile and bowed at me before focusing on Rennie. "Would you mind coming with me? I'd like your opinion on a... delicate matter." He threw a glance at me. "Madam."

"Of course." Rennie turned towards me and paused. "Stay here. I'll be back soon."

For heaven's sake, where would I go? I didn't like his domineering tone, but I nodded, nevertheless. He glanced at me again before disappearing below deck. I shook my head. What could happen to me on the deck filled with people? Every passageway on the ship was full of passengers and members of the crew.

The beauty of the sea was capturing my attention again when a whiff of expensive male cologne reached me.

"Monia." Edward stood next to me, handsome and elegant as usual in all his golden glory. I almost chuckled, thinking of the nurse's description of him.

"Edward!" I couldn't help the note of reproach in my voice. "I've been searching for you. What happened in the castle?"

He removed his tall hat, and the breeze shuffled his blond hair. "I apologise on Sandro's behalf. He saw your... friend and decided it was better not to be seen by him."

I pressed my lips together. "But why?"

He exhaled. "Your parents don't want you to meet Sandro."

Well, thank you. "So I gathered."

"Your friend is here to keep you away from him, I guess."

"Why?" I kept repeating myself, but no one was giving me any answers, and my questions were always the same.

He tossed a glance over his shoulder. "Sandro wants to talk to you about that. He'll be in Tunis tomorrow. Please, do what you can to be alone." With an elegant bow, he went to turn, but I took his arm. A rather bold gesture, but I was going mad, and I wasn't sure I wanted to follow his instructions without some explanation. His eyes widened, but he didn't withdraw his arm.

"I searched for you," I said. "They said there isn't any Mr Edward Marston on board."

"Marston? Who's Marston?" he said, brow furrowing. "It's Morrison, my dear. Now, if you'll excuse me, I have a quite urgent matter to attend to." He slid out of my grip with a quick bow.

"Wait, how do you communicate with Sandro?" I asked his retreating back.

He ignored me, hurrying through the crowd of passengers with the agility of an eel. I glanced in the direction where Rennie had disappeared before following Edward. A group of passengers came out of the stairs, and I had to make my way through wide skirts and people chatting.

"Excuse me." I elbowed my way out of the crowd, but it was wasted energy. I lost sight of Edward. Dash it.

I huffed. I was infatuated with Sandro, but not stupid. The whole affair was more tangled than a pretzel. But there was at least one thing I could do immediately. Grabbing a fistful of my skirt, I strode along the corridor and rushed down the stairs to the reception area. The same young lady I'd seen the other night greeted me with a nervous smile.

"Madam, can I help you?" she asked.

A little breathless, I put my hands on the desk. "Would

you please check if there's a passenger named Edward Morrison on board?"

Her scowl didn't bode well, but she opened the register and skimmed through it. "Morrison... I'm sorry, madam, but there isn't a... oh, no, wait. Yes, Mr Edward Morrison, cabin two-four-six."

I exhaled. "Thank you."

The first number of a cabin corresponded to a level on the ship. So two-four-six meant deck number two. As the SS *Florentia* sailed deeper into the Mediterranean Sea, more passengers rushed to the main deck to admire the view. I had to walk upstream, once again making my way through elegant ladies and too-perfumed gentlemen. Why did some people perfume themselves like that? Rennie, for example—why was I thinking of him? And what was the obsession with his scent?

Shaking my head at my own silliness, I took a corridor on the right and slowed my pace. Cabin two-four-six was tucked in a corner. Edward must have a spectacular view of the sea from that spot.

I knocked on the door, racking my brain for a plausible excuse to talk to him. But then again, I didn't need any excuse. He hadn't answered my questions. "Edw—"

The door was pulled open, and a dark-haired woman came into view. "Good morning," she said, arching a brow. Her words sounded like a question.

Confound it. I hadn't thought Edward could be married.

"Good morning. I'm Miss Monia Fitzwilliam and I was looking for Mr Edward Morrison."

"My husband isn't here at the moment." Her gaze roamed over me. "Why do you want to see him, may I ask?"

"I just wanted to... thank him for dancing with me. He's the most agile dancer I've ever had the honour to dance with." Oops! Of all the things I could have said, I chose the least appropriate one.

"I beg your pardon!" Mrs Morrison's expression became pinched with annoyance. "What are you talking about?"

I wrung my hands. "Well, a few nights ago, he was, ahem, kind enough to dance with me."

"Was he now?" She tilted her head.

"I'm afraid I've taken too much of your time. Don't let me keep you." I turned on my heels and cowardly sprinted away as fast as my petticoats allowed.

Mrs Morrison said something I didn't catch, and I cursed my lack of judgement. If I'd put Edward in an uncomfortable position with his wife, he might decide to stop helping me. If he were helping me. But it wasn't my fault either if he'd disappeared, pretending not to hear me. The whole situation was quite confusing. I groaned inwardly when Rennie swept into view after I rounded a corner. He marched towards me, broad shoulders swaying.

"What are you doing here?" we asked together.

His expression tightened. "I asked you to please stay on the deck. But you left to wander around."

"No. You *ordered* me to stay on the deck. It's different." I went to sidestep him, but he mirrored my moves, blocking me.

"What were you doing on deck two?"

"Nothing of importance." I was being harsh, but if he trusted me and told me everything he knew about Sandro, I wouldn't be so unreasonable. So it was really all his fault. Yes, I was being a cow, but, oh well, the damage was already done.

"I need to know where you are and what you plan to do at any moment. It's not only my job, but, as I told you, I care about your safety, and there are two crazy men on board." His voice rose.

"I was never alone. There were always people around."

"But not me."

"You're overreacting as usual," I said, jabbing a finger at him. "Nothing happened."

"You keep sneaking off on me."

I opened my mouth but then shut it. Because he was right.

"Where did you go?" he asked through gritted teeth.

"To chat with Edward, the man I danced with the other night, but he wasn't in his cabin and I spoke with his wife. That's all." I tilted my chin up, trying to gather my dignity. "Well, now I'm returning to my cabin to freshen up, if that's all right with you." I sauntered off without waiting for his reply.

The low growl he released haunted me as I walked

towards my own cabin. I wasn't sure what game I was playing, but I was sure I wasn't winning it.

SIX

THE COMBINATION OF too many questions filling my mind and so much free time wasn't a good one.

I'd spent the past two days thinking about Sandro, Edward, Rennie, and my parents without finding any connection. How had Sandro found me on board a ship? And if he'd been to Lisbon, how was he going to Tunis? Was he travelling on another cruise ship? Following me? Did he have a private ship of his own?

Detective Norton hadn't discovered anything about the mysterious man who had attacked us or the elusive Scot, and I hadn't spoken much with Rennie, not because I was avoiding him. He was busy with Detective Norton. Anyway, my lack of communication with him turned out to be a problem because the nausea was back with a vengeance.

As we approached Tunis, which sparkled with its

blinding white houses and blue roofs, I was left with no choice but to ask Rennie for a sip of the green potion. A little shiver of dread ran up the back of my neck when I knocked on his door, the memory of the attack still fresh. Heck, the bruise was still there on my ribs to remind me of that kick.

"Rennie?" I said.

No answer.

I hadn't seen him in the dining hall, and he didn't like to stay on the deck and watch the view unless he was following me. Perhaps he was with Norton. Or was he being attacked again? I tried the knob. The door inched inwards.

"Rennie?" I called, sticking my head into the cabin.

No noise. The good news was that he wasn't being attacked. I pushed the door open.

The bed was made. His clothes were neatly folded on the chair. His shoes sparkled with polish and were put aside in a corner. Even the pencils on the writing desk were arranged in a neat line. Military order if I'd ever seen it.

I stepped inside. I could have a very quick look around and search for the green potion without having to ask him anything.

I loitered on the threshold. Rummaging through someone else's room wasn't a decent thing to do. I should wait for Rennie and ask him. But in my defence, the little game of lies we'd been playing had put me in a tight spot.

We both had secrets, and I wanted to see Sandro. So I felt authorised to sneak into Rennie's room. Also, the nausea was becoming unbearable. I needed the green serum now. Sorry, Rennie.

A thrill of excitement made me giggle. I had more questions than ever about Sandro's and Rennie's secrets, but solving the mystery and sneaking around were fun. Finally, I was doing something dangerous and thrilling.

The click of the door shutting behind me sounded like thunder in the small room. I tiptoed to the nightstand and pulled open the drawer. A bunch of letters tied with a red ribbon lay on the bottom. There was a document folded in a corner. I perked up. The elegant, neat writing on the piece of paper belonged to my father.

The curiosity was causing my breath to hitch. Should I read it or not? Leave or stay? The good Monia my parents had raised said to leave. But the naughty Monia, who'd been lied to, said to stay. I was through with being polite. I hated being lied to.

The document was soft to the touch, as if it had been handled and unfolded many times. My hands shook as I unrolled it. The piece of paper was a contract between Father and Rennie.

Rennie had been hired to escort me during the trip around the Mediterranean Sea. Nothing new so far. I pressed my lips together as I read the list of clauses Rennie had to observe while working for my father. He had to take an oath that he would never, under any circumstances, touch me inappropriately, approach me with indecorous manners, or develop any romantic interest towards me, on pain of being expelled from the Royal Occult Bureau—the royal what? What in Hades was that?—and of being flogged until unconsciousness took him.

What? I wasn't sure if I understood it correctly. Flogged?

What pile of horse dung was that? No one had been punished by flogging in England since... well, I had no idea, but it sounded mediaeval, to say the least. Also, how could Rennie avoid developing a romantic interest in someone? If he was attracted to someone, he couldn't stop it, could he? And my goodness, he would be flogged. It was absolutely barbaric.

I folded the piece of paper and put it back in the drawer. If my parents didn't want Rennie as my suitor, as I'd originally thought, then what was I doing here with him? Why were they against Sandro as my suitor? The only explanation was Rennie was protecting me from the assassins who wanted Sandro dead. But was a cruise a good idea? I'd be safer in the country where I could have as many bodyguards as my parents wanted. Unless the assassins were in England. My head was about to explode. Nothing made sense.

A vial of green potion rolled towards me when I shuffled the envelopes. I took it and slid it into my pocket, a hint of guilt stabbing my chest.

More confused than ever, I exited the cabin and shut

the door behind me. The more I searched for answers, the more questions I found. I paused in front of Rennie's cabin, rolling my bottom lip between my teeth and patting the vial in my pocket. Footsteps padded from the other side of the corridor. I shivered when Rennie walked towards me, suspicion tightening his face.

"What are you doing here?" he asked.

I straightened. "I wanted to tell you that... I don't feel well," I said in a moment of inspiration. "I'll stay in my cabin, sleeping."

"What's the problem? Is it the pain in the ribs?"

"No, it's another thing. A private thing. A thing I don't wish to share."

A little crease appeared between his eyebrows. "Fair enough. Is there anything I can do for you?"

Oh, bother. Guilt stabbed me again. He was so sweet while I'd just rummaged through his things. "No, thank you. I'm going to my cabin."

"I'll be here if you need me."

"Thank you." I could feel the weight of his stare on me all the way down the corridor.

As usual, the SS *Florentia* took a long time to dock in the port of Tunis. I paced in my cabin, rolling the vial between my hands. All I had to do was wait for the right moment and sneak out of my cabin without Rennie being the wiser. It'd be the last time I sneaked out without telling him. I'd talk to Sandro, and that would be the end of it.

As my stomach groaned with nausea, I uncorked the

vial and took a sip, my hands trembling with guilt and seasickness.

"Monia?" The knock on the door caused me to jolt, and I swallowed more green potion than I meant. Lord, it burned. I coughed and beat a fist against my chest, spitting green drops.

"Monia?" The voice belonged to Rennie, of course.

The potion was so sweet that I pulled out my tongue. The liquid burned all the way down to my stomach like strong sherry. I wiped my mouth with a handkerchief.

"Yes." I put the vial in my pocket and opened the door, my stomach burning. I kept my distance from him and opened it only a crack, in case he could smell the green serum.

Tall and intimidating, he towered over me. "How do you feel? Do you really want to stay here? We've arrived in Tunis."

My head spun. I didn't have to fake the moment of dizziness that took me. "Yes. I prefer to stay here." Even my voice sounded weak. Perfect. Or maybe not.

His posture slackened, as if he hadn't expected my illness to be real. He craned his neck to look at me. "Do you want me to call the doctor?"

I pressed the handkerchief to my mouth. "No. I'll stay in bed and rest. I'm sure I'll feel better soon."

"Do you want a cup of tea?"

"I'm going to sleep, so no, thank you." Guilt would be the death of me.

He nodded, studying me. "I'll come in later to see how

you're faring. I'll bring you a repast and something to drink if you want."

"No." It came out too quickly. "I'm going to lock myself in and put a chair against the door as you told me. I just need some sleep."

He eyed me again as silence stretched between us. "All right. Let me know if you need anything."

"I will. Thank you."

He gave a curt nod and left. I wouldn't call him a friend, but I didn't want him to be flogged nearly to death because of me. He might be brusque sometimes, but he was a good man.

"I'm sorry," I whispered to his retreating figure.

I tottered to the bed, wondering if I should stay here for real. But I wanted to see Sandro, and I wanted answers. After half an hour, my head felt clear and my stomach stopped burning enough to allow me to stand without staggering.

The straw hat I donned covered half of my face, giving me some privacy. I chose a dull brown dress I hadn't worn during the cruise so far. Hopefully, no one would pay me too much attention. Keeping my head down, I headed towards the main deck and the gangplank, blending in with the crowd of people eager to see Tunis. I loitered before leaving the ship as I waited for a large group of passengers.

Tunis stretched out in front of me with its sandy shore and gleaming white houses. A wall built with limestone slabs rose to the right, casting a shadow on the golden sand.

As my dizziness subsided, I smiled at the lovely city. Coming here hadn't been such a bad idea.

I gaped at the magnificently tall palm trees bordering the High Road. Signs in French and Arabic pointed out the names of palaces and ancient places. Even the scents filling the air were a combination of French and Arabic traditions. There was the rich, buttery smell of fresh croissants wafting out of a bakery, and the spicy fragrance of couscous cooked with meat.

Visiting a city on my own, without the hindrance of the giggling tourists and the shouting guide—or a sulky bodyguard—had its charms. I sat on a bench in a park and enjoyed the sunlight warming my skin, wondering how Sandro would find me. In Oxford, I wouldn't be able to walk on my own without a chaperone. My parents wouldn't allow it. But here, I could simply be myself. I closed my eyes and relaxed for the first time in days.

"May I join you?"

I would recognise Sandro's musical voice in a yelling crowd in the middle of a storm.

I flung my eyes open and sucked in a deep breath. Sandro was standing in front of me, tall, dark, and as breathtakingly handsome as I remembered him. No, he was even more handsome than I remembered. He was divine. The man embodied every fantasy and dream I'd ever had of the perfect man for me, from the limpid blue of his eyes to the fine bones of his cheeks and his musical voice. He was simply perfect.

"Sandro," I whispered, my pulse spiking.

He removed his tall hat, freeing the mop of dark hair that brushed his face. "I've been longing to see you again, sweet Monia." He sat next to me, his gaze studying my face. A whiff of his citrus scent teased my nostrils. "My goodness, you're so beautiful that I can't breathe. May I hug you? I've dreamt of you so often."

I wrapped my arms around his neck and held him tightly, burying my face in the crook of his neck. His skin was soft under my touch, and a sense of calm washed over me.

"I missed you so much, my darling." He stroked my hair gently.

I snuggled closer to him. His touch sent a thrill down my spine. "I missed you, too."

We remained there, holding each other for a while. All the questions I meant to ask him were trapped in my mouth.

"May I kiss you?" he asked, caressing my hair. "I wished to kiss you that night in the garden before your mother started screaming."

Rennie's face flashed through my mind. "I don't know."

He laughed. "What answer is that?" He caressed my cheek again, and my body slackened. "One kiss."

He whispered my name softly before pressing his mouth against mine and slipping his tongue between my teeth. Emotions spilt heat within me, like the energy that charged the air before a storm. He moved his mouth over mine gently, and although I wasn't an expert in kissing, he mastered the technique beautifully. His tongue touched mine right as I wanted. He balanced strength and passion like an artist. It was the perfect kiss—heavenly and passionate. Exactly as I'd imagined it to be.

Brushing my cheeks with his knuckles, he broke the kiss. The blue in his eyes had disappeared, swallowed by a glossy black that was spilling even into the white.

Blimey. I blinked and rubbed my temple.

"Are you all right?" he asked, caressing my shoulder.

"It's nothing." I gazed up. His eyes were blue again. Odd. Maybe the darn green potion was to blame.

"You have a peculiar taste. What is it?" Maybe it was my imagination, but there was a note of anger in his voice.

I put a hand on my mouth. Dash it. Why hadn't I brushed my teeth before leaving the ship? "I took something for my seasickness. It was killing me. Maybe that's it."

His eyes glinted, and a sudden harshness tensed his features. "It doesn't matter." He stroked my cheek again, but with a certain stiffness.

"Sandro, what happened? Why don't my parents want me to be with you? And what does Edward have to do with anything?" I wanted to ask more questions, but I stopped myself. "You left me without a word. Then my parents sent me to Southampton to board a darn ship. I don't understand what's happening. Nobody tells me anything."

"Because we want to protect you." A flush coloured his smooth skin. "Monia, my kingdom is being threatened by anarchists. They tried to kill me more than once, even in

England. Those assassins know no limits. I had to leave. I don't want anything to happen to you because of me. Your parents were terrified you might be hurt because of me." Each time he touched me, my spine wilted, my mind fogged, and my determination to seek answers faded. It was like a spell. "I agreed it was too dangerous to stay with you. I wanted to see you one last time, but for safety reasons, I had to flee."

"Will I see you again?" My body wasn't obeying me. I wanted to know more about the danger he was facing, but his touch was distracting me.

"Of course. Very soon." He brushed his lips over my ear, sending a shot of desire straight to my core. "But please stay on the SS *Florentia*. The ship is safe." He kissed me again, but not with passion.

Was the green serum so disgusting for him? Speaking of which, the dizziness was back.

"I have to go." He kissed the tip of my nose and shot a glance behind me. Whatever he saw caused him to stiffen. "See you soon, my angel. I'll be thinking of you every moment until we meet again." Goodness, he ran away. Fast.

I waved, but I was having trouble keeping my eyes open. I mumbled a farewell, my tongue growing numb. As he became an indistinguishable figure in the crowd of people walking along the pavement, another figure became very distinctive. Rennie was striding towards me in all his red-hot anger. Even from a distance, I could tell he was furious.

Nostrils flaring, he stopped in front of me. "What is the meaning of this?"

I laughed. I couldn't help it. My head spun, I wanted to sleep, and I wasn't sure why I found his words so terribly funny. "You're so furious." I giggled. Somewhere, in a remote corner of my mind, I felt ashamed of myself.

"Do you find my anger funny? What is that?" He took a sniff and held my face and examined it, brow furrowing. Then his eyes flared wide with what looked like fear. "Bloody hell." His rough hands patted me down in a rather rude manner.

I swatted them. "Hey. Stop that." Despite my words, I giggled again.

He didn't listen. "I knew it." He fished out the vial from my pocket.

I was expecting him to become even angrier, but his face morphed into sheer panic. "How long ago did you take it?"

"A while." I wanted to sleep, laugh, and cast up my accounts in whatever order happened to come first. "I'm so tired."

His arms wrapped around me as he picked me up. "Don't sleep now. Not yet. We must get back to the ship."

"Why?"

"You need help. Walk with me, Monia."

His warm body was solid and reassuring. I found myself leaning against him as he half-dragged, half-carried me towards the ship.

"I told you not to drink too much green serum." His tone was concerned rather than accusatory.

"I didn't mean to drink more than a sip." A hiccup escaped me. "But you knocked on my door and gave me a fright. I swallowed more than I wanted." My head was so heavy that it bobbed back and forth on its own.

He nudged me when I stopped talking. "Keep talking and keep moving. Say something. Don't fall asleep."

"I don't know what to say." I shuffled my feet forwards. A quick laugh shook me.

The impossibly blue sky of Tunis seemed to fall on me, and the palm trees bent towards the ground. The white houses were closing in on me, and the road stretched and contracted in front of me. I had no idea how far we were from the ship, or if it was hot or cold. Sweat trickled down my neck, but goosebumps pebbled my skin. The only thing I was fully aware of was Rennie's body pressing against mine and the strange pleasure it was giving me.

"Tell me what you did in my room," he said, a desperate note in his voice.

Another giggle came out of me. "What's the Royal Occult Bureau? Funnily enough, it sounds familiar."

He paused, his muscles tensing under his clothes. "You read my contract."

I tilted my head up towards him. The only clear features on his face were his big emerald eyes burning down at me. The rest was an indistinct blur of harsh lines and masculine features.

"It's a terrible contract if you ask me. I'm ashamed of

what my father made you sign." Somehow, my hand was on his chest, exploring the hard wall of muscles. "I don't want you to be flogged because of me." Giggle. Giggle. Giggle. "But then again, there's no chance you'll become romantically interested in me. That's ridiculous."

He resumed walking, taking almost all my weight. "Why do you think so?"

"I'm not your type. You don't like me." His heart was thumping underneath my palm, a steady pounding that calmed me.

"To start with, I told you I find you pretty." There was a strained note in his voice as he sped up.

I waved a dismissive hand, resting my head on the crook of his neck. "That's only my body. You don't like *me*, who I am."

"You're wrong." He gathered me in his arms, fully carrying me now. The fact that he was holding me distracted me from his words.

"You're carrying me," I said, resting my cheek against his hard chest as I touched his neck. What a strong neck he had. Kissable. Biteable.

"Don't make yourself too comfortable. I'm going to drop you to your feet as soon as we're onboard. You need to walk and move."

The subtle up-and-down movement suggested we were walking along the gangplank. The familiar wood-polish scent of the ship reached me. True to his word, Rennie put me down on the main deck.

"I'll take you to my cabin, all right? I need to lower

your temperature. You're burning up." He coiled an arm around my waist and led me down the stairs.

"My temperature?" Now that he mentioned it, heat was bursting out of me. Sweat trickled down my back. The fabric of my shirt chafed my sensitive skin, and my drawers were wet, and not the good kind of wet. "You're right. I am a bit hot."

"It'll be worse in a few minutes unless we take care of it." He actually gathered me in his arms again and carried me below deck. I sighed. I quite liked being in his arms. He nudged me with his shoulder. "Don't fall asleep, please, darling."

Darling? I forced my eyelids up. He was breathing hard, and even his pulse was racing. "Darling," I muttered. I liked that.

The semidarkness in his cabin was a welcome change from the brightness of the day. He kicked the door shut and then we were alone. Only him, me, and my rising temperature. We shouldn't be alone in a locked room. But I didn't really care.

He took my face and angled it, so that we stared into each other's eyes. "Monia, I'm sorry, but I have to undress you." His fingers worked on the buttons of my shirt.

"Rennie, what are you doing?" I didn't have the energy to swat his fingers away and to be honest, I liked how he was unbuttoning my shirt.

"Trying to save your life." He untied my overskirt and petticoats with speed and efficiency.

The clothes slipped down my body and pooled at my

feet until I stood in my chemise and drawers. The moment the cool air hit my clammy skin, I sighed in relief. "Ah, thank you for that. I need it. Sod propriety."

"Lie here." Rennie picked me up again and laid me down on his bed. "I'll be right back."

"Can I sleep now?" I wiggled my toes; they were burning too.

"No, not yet. I want you to sing until I'm back, all right? Sing, Monia. Sing."

I chuckled, but it was too hot to keep laughing. The only song I could think of was *The Lights o' London*. I didn't fully remember all the words, so I made them up. My voice echoed in the cabin, and the more I heard it, the more I wanted to laugh and sleep. I was so tired.

"The devil, were you singing? You gave me such a fright!" Rennie was carrying a bucket so big that he staggered on his feet. "It sounded like you were being butchered."

I closed my eyes. Exhaustion burned through me. "I thought I was all right."

There were noises as Rennie muttered curses under his breath and fussed around me. A wave of freezing cold caused me to open my eyes again right when I was slipping into unconsciousness. The chill was both a relief and a shock. I gazed down. Ice cubes covered my body. Rennie was placing them with surgical precision on my chest, belly, knees, and wrists.

"Drink this." He lifted my head gently, holding a vial with a pale-yellow liquid.

"What is it?"

"An antidote of sort."

The potion didn't have any remarkable taste. It could be lukewarm water, but the burning heat consuming me diminished a little.

"Better?" he asked, rubbing two ice cubes over my temples. He seemed to ignore the fact that my chemise was soaked and plastered to my breasts, and that with the sudden cold, my nipples were two hard peaks, pointing up at him. But I was too tired to care.

"Better," I said, letting out a sigh.

My head stopped spinning. As he cooled my temples with the ice cubes, moving them in slow circles, I moaned, squirming a little. He ran an ice cube down my neck and collarbone, and up again. The little devil sneaked down the valley between my breasts. He swallowed hard and retrieved the fleeing ice cube, brushing my wet breasts in the process. With my sensitive skin, the gentle touch intensified, and I let out another moan. There was no mistaking the nature of it. Not pain, but pleasure.

"Don't move too much." He brushed a lock of my hair from my face. "The ice will drop your temperature. Stay still."

"Do it again," I whispered.

"No, darling, you aren't well." He caressed my cheek with the ice cube. Drops of water slid down my neck.

"I want it. Touch me. You have my permission."

He let out a nervous chuckle. "We'll discuss that again when you're well." He kept stroking my body with the ice cubes, shuffling them around and replacing them when they melted, but he didn't touch me again, and I was growing weaker.

"Can I sleep now?" I slurred, fighting the heaviness of my eyelids and the funny taste in my mouth.

"Yes, you can." He caressed my hair and cheeks. "I'll watch over you."

SEVEN

A WARM BLANKET was wrapped around me when I woke up. The ice cubes were gone, but the bed sheets were dry, and I wasn't burning with fever.

Slowly, I sat up and suppressed a gasp, clenching the blanket tightly. Rennie was asleep on the floor in front of the door, curled up on his side. As the weight of what I'd done sank in, my cheeks flamed with shame. I'd laughed and giggled while Rennie had been trying to help me. I'd asked him to touch me. I'd insisted on it. He must have thought I'd behaved like an idiot.

My chemise had been swapped for a crisp white shirt that, judging by the clean, soapy scent, belonged to him. My skin was still raw, and the starched fabric chafed my nipples. Hades, even sober, the thought of Rennie touching me sent a thrill of excitement down my neck. The green potion wasn't the reason I wanted him to touch me. Was I betraying Sandro?

"Monia." He was on his feet in a heartbeat. Hades, I hadn't seen him moving. "How do you feel? Let me touch your forehead." Before I could answer, he put his big, rough hand on my forehead. The contact caused my temperature to rise again. "Thank God, you're all right." He sagged onto the edge of the bed and rubbed his eyes. "I was so worried."

I opened my mouth to say... I wasn't sure what. "What happened? Why did you have to cover me in ice?"

"Your temperature was rising due to the green serum. Unless a doctor gives you the correct dose for your body, it can poison you. It's more dangerous when injected into the body, but drinking it in large doses isn't safe. You developed a high fever that frightened me to death. Please don't do it again." He closed his hand around mine and rubbed my knuckles with his thumb. "And don't steal anything from my room."

His thumb was distracting and soothing. My breath came out quicker. I liked it when he caressed me. The sensation was different compared to Sandro's touch, wilder and more shocking, but pleasant, nevertheless. He could be gentle with his hands when he wanted to be.

I lowered my gaze, avoiding his intense scrutiny. "I'm sorry. I didn't mean it. I just wanted some green potion, but you weren't in your cabin and..."

"And curiosity won."

I nodded, sighing as he kept stroking my knuckles.

"You could've died." The reproach in his voice was hard to miss. It thickened the air between us.

"You could have told me about the contract." It was unfair of me to bring it up, but why hadn't he told me about the contract?

"So is it my fault now?" He stopped rubbing my knuckles with his thumb.

"I'm not saying that. No, wait. I'm saying that. I'm joking." I threw my free hand up. "Fine. I'm sorry. For everything. All my fault. Even for... you know."

"What?" He tilted his head.

"You know." I waved around.

"I don't understand. You have to be more clear."

I sighed, but he kept stroking my knuckles, soothing my nerves. "For having been inappropriate with you."

"You needn't worry." He flashed a cheeky grin. "You were adorable."

"And naked." I arched my eyebrows.

"No, you had your chemise on."

A scoff escaped me. "It's curious. When the back of my dress had a few buttons unfastened, you said I was naked. When I was wearing only my wet chemise in your bed, you said I was dressed."

He shrugged. "Curious."

"Did you remove my chemise?" I asked, inching closer to him.

"It was soaked. But I had my eyes closed. Most of the time. I barely saw anything and—"

I hit him with the pillow, and he barked a rich, deep laugh. "You rascal."

Laughing, he brought my hand up and kissed it. I

stilled. When he laughed, he was completely different. His eyes brightened, his tense muscles relaxed, and he radiated charm. I laughed too until my belly was shaking.

He kissed my hand again, a quick brush of his lips against my skin. "What did you do in Tunis?"

Oops. I slid my hand out of his. "Can't a girl take a walk?"

"Not if the girl is Sanctimonia Fitzwilliam and I'm in charge of her protection under the punishment of being flogged. As you know." He gave me a pointed look.

Guilt roared back to life. He'd be tortured if something happened to me. "I admit I've been selfish. I don't like the idea of you having to suffer because of me. Had I known, I wouldn't have left you behind."

"Yes, you would have." He smirked, flashing his straight teeth. "You don't have to take care of me. It's the other way around." The kindness in his voice melted a frozen spot in my chest that I didn't know was that cold.

"I'll tell you what I did in Tunis if you tell me what the Royal Occult Bureau is," I whispered. "Is it the department where my father works?"

After a long pause, he opened his mouth, but the knock on the door shut him up.

"Steele?" Detective Norton spoke from the other side. "I'm sorry to trouble you, but it's urgent. I need to talk to you."

"I'm coming," Rennie shouted towards the door. "Quick, hide," he whispered to me, straightening.

"What—" Right. There was no need to ruin my reputation by being discovered half-naked in my *cousin's* cabin. Wrapped in the blanket, I tiptoed towards a corner where Norton wouldn't see me.

After I hid in the dark spot, Rennie opened the door. "What happened?" he asked, his voice a little breathy.

"It's Mrs Francis, the woman who was attacked by the phantom Scot. She's disappeared. The members of the crew are sure she returned on board yesterday." Norton paused, his breathing coming out in raspy sounds. "She was seen by many witnesses in the dining hall. Her husband confirmed she was on board, but when he woke up in the middle of the night to take a drink of water, she wasn't in the room. He didn't worry about her immediately, thinking she must've got up for some reason. But this morning, she wasn't in the cabin, and no one has seen her."

"Dammit." Rennie scrubbed a hand on his unshaven chin.

I suppressed a gasp. I hadn't taken Mrs Francis seriously when she'd described the attack from the hunky Scotsman. And now she was missing.

"I know it's not your job," Norton said, "but would you mind giving me a hand? I'm doing everything alone here, and it's become a bit overwhelming. I don't usually need any help. Nothing has ever happened on board until now."

"Of course. I'll help you search the ship. Give me five minutes," Rennie said.

Norton must have nodded because his footsteps echoed from the corridor.

"I want to help," I said after Rennie shut the door.

He pointed at a chair. "Your clothes are over there. They should be dry." There was a moment of heated silence between us. Likely, he was thinking of when he'd taken those clothes off me. He cleared his throat and rubbed his chest, drawing attention to a triangle of golden skin visible between the lapels of his shirt. "I'll leave you alone, so you can change. Then we'll search the ship together if you feel strong enough."

"Thank you. I'm all right." Not that he hadn't seen the whole of me already.

He opened the door and paused. "Our conversation isn't over."

"No, it's not."

TWENTY MINUTES LATER, I'd changed clothes twice. The dress I'd been wearing yesterday stank of dust, sweat, and green potion. So I slid it on to walk to my room and then changed into a fresh morning dress. Rennie followed my every move, leaving me alone only when I had to undress. I didn't protest. He was risking his life for me, and I'd nearly died yesterday. When I was ready, I left the cabin and walked next to him in the passageway. His harsh expression softened when he gazed at me and the dark-blue dress hugging my body and giving the illusion I had hips.

"What did you do in Tunis?" he asked without preamble.

I exhaled and reminded myself of his contract. "I met Sandro."

"What?" He skidded to an abrupt halt.

I winced. "Edward told me Sandro was in Tunis, and I met him. We had a chat and nothing happened."

"Aside from you nearly dying."

"That was my doing. Sandro didn't hurt me."

"What did he tell you?" He had the tone of a copper.

I shrugged. "Not much. He said a band of anarchists wanted him dead, and that was why he had to leave."

He shook his head. "Don't meet him again."

"Why?" I was growing tired of asking it.

"Because he's dangerous. I don't know what he meant with the cock-and-bull story he spun, but he's a menace. Stay away from him." He blew out a sharp breath. "I can't believe it. How did he find you?"

"He never hurt me, and I don't think he was lying." I wanted to sound offended, but his fear doused my anger and planted doubts in my mind. "I don't understand why my parents and you are so convinced he's a scoundrel."

"Please." He put his hands on my shoulders and stared at me. Pain etched his features. "Please trust me."

"But you give me no reason to doubt Sandro."

"Please," he said again, swallowing. "I need you to trust me. Don't run away again."

What could I do? I didn't want him to get hurt because of me, even though I didn't understand why he didn't tell me anything. I nodded. "I promise."

His shoulders dipped as he pulled me into his arms. "Thank you."

I sagged against him, resting my head on his chest. Being hugged felt terribly good.

He caressed the top of my head, muttering, "Thank you." When he released me, he fiddled with the collar of his shirt.

I brushed a speck of dust from my sleeve. "Great."

"Yes." He straightened his jacket.

"You're welcome."

"Good. You're welcome too."

I cleared my throat. "Where do we start?" I asked, tugging at my bodice and hoping it would make my breasts look bigger.

He peeled his gaze off me. "Mrs Francis's cabin. I want to talk to her husband."

"Do you think the mysterious Scotsman is the culprit?"

A pained expression scrunched up his face. "I don't know. Nothing makes sense on this bloody ship. Two attackers disappear into thin air while there are two thousand people on board. No one saw anything. None of the Scots on board fit the description Mrs Francis gave us. The attacker might not have been a Scot at all, but how many six-foot-six tall, red-haired men with broad shoulders and thick legs, and wearing a kilt can be on a bloody ship?"

"You're right. I, for one, would have noticed such a strapping man." I chuckled, but he didn't join me.

The glare he shot at me could have broken a porthole. "That's a good point." It didn't sound like he meant it.

"Maybe Mrs Francis lied about the Scot," I said. "Maybe she made him up because she wanted attention? Make her husband jealous?"

"That's another good point." He worked his jaw.

I knocked on Mr Francis's door. "Mr Francis? It's Miss Monia Fitzwilliam and Mr Rennie Steele here. Detective Norton sent us to help find your wife."

The door was flung open. A distressed and dishevelled Mr Francis greeted me. His dark hair stuck out in every direction, and his eyes were red-rimmed. "Do you have any news about Mildred?"

"I'm afraid not. But Rennie and I are here to help." I gave him an encouraging smile. "Can you tell us what happened?"

He repeated what Norton had told Rennie, that Mrs Francis had gone to bed last night, but in the morning, she wasn't in her cabin.

"Did she tell you anything about her attacker?" Rennie asked in his copper tone, as if he were used to interrogating people. *Because he is.* The thought came unbidden from some corner of my mind.

The Royal Occult Bureau. Coppers. Military order. A sharp ache slashed through my head, and whatever thought I was chasing in my mind was gone. Still, for a split second, I grasped something about the Royal Occult Bureau. I'd heard about it before. I focused. No, nothing. Another pang shot through my head, and the thought was lost. As if on cue, the scar on my wrist flared up, and I scratched it.

Rennie put a hand on my shoulder. "Are you all right?"

I nodded, tugging at my sleeve.

Mr Francis produced a handkerchief from his pocket and patted his sweaty face. "We had a furious row about her Scottish attacker. She seemed..." He glanced around and opened the door wider. "Would you mind coming in?"

We slid into the wide cabin—it was twice as big as mine with an impressive king-size bed—and he shut the door.

"What were you saying?" I said gently when he tormented his handkerchief, pulling it between his hands.

"Well, she didn't seem distressed at all. A man had attacked her, and she was swooning over him, saying how handsome he'd looked, how strapping he'd been, and how he'd spoken with bold words that she'd loved. I scolded her and told her that wasn't the behaviour of a woman in distress. She became angry and said I didn't understand her. These were the last words we exchanged." His voice cracked. "And now she's probably with him."

I grimaced. Poor chap. He might be right.

"Do you think she knew where to find the Scot?" Rennie asked, unfazed by the man's distress.

Mr Francis lifted a shoulder. "Where else could she be if not with him?" He shook his head. "She felt sick a few weeks ago before we left Southampton. The doctor said her heart was having problems, but she dismissed the diagnosis, saying it was simply her nerves if she didn't feel well and that she wanted to take the cruise all the same. But I don't think she felt sick. Someone would have found her by now. No, she's with him, somewhere on the ship." His dark eyes hardened.

"Well, that's an interesting theory," I said, strolling around. A lurid Gothic novel lay on the night table. *The Laird's Captive*, the title read. A hunky, red-haired Scot in a kilt filled the cover. His thick locks of hair fell over his piercing blue eyes. Interesting.

Rennie's gaze followed mine, and he frowned. "Thank you for your time, Mr Francis. We'll take a look around and tell you if we find your wife."

"And the Scot. Don't forget the devilishly handsome Scot," he said with enough fire to boil water. "Find him, and you'll find her. Foolish woman."

"We won't forget about him." I smiled and opened the door.

We left poor Mr Francis and headed towards Norton's office.

"Do you think she found him? The Scot?" I asked, stepping closer to Rennie.

"Or he found her."

"Did you see the novel?"

He scratched his unshaven chin, and a fleeting thought about how the stubble would feel on my skin crossed my mind. "Yes, and I don't like it."

"Well, that proves it. She made the Scot up, or her imagination played a trick on her."

He clicked his tongue. "I hope it's something as simple as that."

"I mean, who doesn't want to be kissed by a Scot like that on the cover?"

If I didn't know better, I'd say Rennie's expression was tightening with jealousy.

After Norton joined us, we knocked on every door on the third level with the help of a few members of the staff. Even other passengers volunteered to search for Mrs Francis when the news about her disappearance spread. Everyone was up and about, looking for the missing woman, but Mrs Francis seemed to have truly vanished. While Norton and Rennie were searching the cabins on the left side of the passageway, I headed towards the other side.

I lost sight of Rennie after I rounded a corner and found myself in front of the theatre. Every day, three different plays were staged. I hadn't seen any, but since I was here, I wanted to take a look. Besides, Mrs Francis might be there, with or without her Scot. The set of double doors opened with a soft swish when I pushed them. The theatre was empty. Only a few lights were on, casting a yellow glow on the red-velvet seats.

"Mrs Francis?" Likely, the staff had already searched the theatre, but it wouldn't hurt to search it again. "It's me, Monia."

I strolled down the shallow stairs towards the stage. It was smaller than the stage of the Royal Theatre in Oxford, but the details of the carved decorations were exquisite.

"Mrs Fr—" I stopped as my foot touched something soft.

Heart in my throat and half-expecting to see Mrs Francis's pale hand sticking out from underneath a seat, I crouched. No. No cold hand or other body parts. It was a blob of a sticky silver substance that glittered in the light from the sconces. I touched it with a finger. It was warm and semi-solid like jelly. Perhaps it was something the actors used for their make-up, but I'd never seen anything like it. The blob was thick and sticky. I had to rub my finger on a handkerchief to clean it off. I had barely time to exit the theatre before Rennie was on me like a bloodhound.

"Where have you been?" he asked, searching my face. "Did you feel sick again?" He cupped my cheek, cutting off what I was about to say. "Did someone hurt you?"

I put my hand on his. "Calm yourself. I simply had a look at the theatre."

His shoulders sagged. "I thought you'd left me again." He wrapped his arms around me and held me close to his body. Twice in a row. I couldn't say I didn't like it. I relaxed in his embrace. It was familiar, but exciting at the same time. As if realising he was touching me, he released me and stepped back.

I shifted my weight. "Any news?"

The tension in his shoulders dissolved as his stance slackened. "No news. I thought Mrs Francis might've felt sick and remained stuck somewhere, but that's not the case. The only explanation for her absence is that she fell overboard. Norton is going to declare an incident as the official reason for her disappearance. Unfortunately, in cases like this, there isn't much else that can be done. If she fell into the sea, recovering her body would be impossible."

"Oh, no." A cold sensation filled my stomach at the thought of poor Mrs Francis falling into the sea. I pressed the stained handkerchief against my chest. "I hope that isn't what happened to her."

Rennie's gaze returned sharp. "What's that?"

"What?" I glanced around.

"That stain." He took my handkerchief, brushing my fingers in the process. A riot of emotions was displayed on his face as he examined the stain. He paled, then his facial muscles hardened. "What's that?" he repeated.

"Something sticky and silver stained my finger, and I removed it with my—"

"Where did you find it?"

"In the theatre."

"Show me." It was an order. But the urgency in his words didn't make me argue.

We strode into the theatre. I led him towards the point in front of the orchestra pit where I'd found the blob.

"It's here—" There was nothing on that spot. It was clean and pristine. I crouched and felt around. "I don't understand. It was here. I swear it. A large blob of silver material."

Rennie crouched next to me, his shoulder brushing mine. "I believe you." He searched the floor and looked underneath the row of seats.

His thorough inspection lasted nearly twenty minutes. And then it dawned on me. He had done that before.

Investigating. It was what he did for a living. He was a copper of some sort. No, he was an investigator of strange events, of occult events.

Another headache struck me. I rubbed my temples, wondering if my little escapade of yesterday had done more damage than I'd thought.

"Do you feel sick?" Rennie was next to me in a flash.

"Just a headache." If I'd told him I was bleeding to death, he would have looked less worried.

"Headache?" He passed a hand over his face.

"Did you discover anything useful?" I asked to distract him.

"Yes." He handed me the handkerchief. "And I have some bad news for you."

EIGHT

WHEN RENNIE HAD said he had bad news for me, I hadn't imagined it would be that bad.

We were approaching Cairo, and apparently, I wasn't allowed to join any groups to visit the city. I wasn't allowed to go anywhere without him. I wasn't allowed to have fun. Rennie had claimed he had 'work' to do in Cairo. Thus, I was supposed to follow him to the City of the Dead where he would blindfold me and take me somewhere he didn't want me to see. How absurd.

He didn't want to leave me alone, even for one moment. We'd spent the day searching the ship for Mrs Francis—without finding anything—and now I was finally in my cabin, finishing washing and changing. I wasn't surprised when a knock came from the door.

I tightened the sash of my dressing gown and tossed my braided hair behind my shoulder. "Rennie," I said, opening the door.

He slipped inside, ignoring me. "Are you going to bed?"

"I'm tired, and I had a quick repast." I didn't shut the door because surely, he was leaving at any moment.

"Right." He removed his jacket and draped it on a chair, remaining in a grey waistcoat and crisp white shirt that enhanced his broad shoulders.

"What are you doing?" I wished my voice didn't sound so husky.

"You can lock the door."

Heat burst from somewhere in my lower belly and crawled up to my neck and cheeks. The worst thing was that I wasn't sure the flare was entirely due to the shock.

"Would you please explain to me your intentions?" I asked, with my back to the open door.

He walked towards me, radiating enough predatory menace to make me step back. "I'm going to sleep in this cabin until further notice." Only a few inches separated us.

He shut the door with one hand and caged me between the door and his strapping body. An entirely foreign sensation burned in the pit of my belly and lower. Had he always been so intense, so charming? His crooked nose wasn't as noticeable as I'd thought at first. If anything, it fit his harsh face and strong jaw and gave him the air of a dangerous scoundrel. And I was having these inappropriate thoughts because...?

"I sleep here tonight," he repeated, stepping back. "Non-negotiable."

I cleared my throat, remembering what Mother had

taught me about etiquette and propriety. Something about never sleeping with a man who wasn't my husband and never starting to shout unless it gave me an advantage. "You can't be serious. This is highly unacceptable."

"It's not the first time I do something unacceptable, and I have a contract, as you know. I'm not going to do anything improper, but I must protect you." His gaze roamed over my pink dressing gown for the briefest of seconds. "Like it or not, I'm staying here, Monia."

I clenched my fist. "You're bossy."

"I've been called worse."

I folded my arms over my chest. "It's because of that silver substance I found, isn't it? What is it? It can't be a coincidence that I find an odd silver thing and you become so incredibly worried about me that you want to sleep here, and threaten to blindfold me."

He shrugged, a cheeky grin stretching his full lips. "Dinosaurs didn't wear transparent pink dressing gowns and went extinct. Is that a coincidence?"

My mouth hung open. "My dressing gown isn't transparent." I wished I'd said something smarter.

He tilted his head. His eyes widened as he studied me. "It is, especially if there's light coming from behind you."

"Bloody hell!" I clamped my hands over my mouth, shame pounding through me. Me? Swearing? "See what you've done? I've never, ever sworn in my entire life."

"There's always a first time, and admit it, it feels so damn good."

Well, he had a point.

"And I didn't threaten to blindfold you," he said, stretching his arms over his head. "I told you exactly what will happen once we're in the City of the Dead."

"And it's for my safety." I hoped he detected the sarcasm in my voice.

He nodded. "Absolutely. Now, shall we go to sleep? Tomorrow is going to be a busy day for both of us." With that, he sat on the floor, his back against the door. "And swearing suits you if you ask me. You look lovely when you say curses. Please curse more often."

"You rascal."

He shook his head. "You can do better than that."

"You... scoundrel."

"Please." He laughed.

I rolled my bottom lip between my teeth, thinking. "Is 'you bastard' good enough?"

He barked a laugh, his chest expanding. "Hell, yes. I love the way you say it."

A storm of emotions was raging inside me, and if I had to be honest with myself, there wasn't only shame. The rules of etiquette had been etched into my brain for as long as I could remember. Letting go of them wasn't easy, but his cocky attitude was charming.

"You shouldn't sleep in my room," I said.

"Good. Excellent. Great. Pity that I have a job to do and I'm not keen on the idea of being flogged." He wasn't joking, of course. "Go to sleep, Monia. I give you my word that I will not touch you."

I let out a breath, admitting defeat. Maybe the fact he

wasn't going to touch me was the cause of the disappointment swelling in my chest.

He heaved a sigh and gazed away. "And step out of the light and cover yourself or keeping my word might be rather difficult." As if realising he'd said something shocking, he clenched his jaw and closed his eyes. "Sleep," he repeated through gritted teeth.

I slid under the quilt and turned off the light, shock leaving me speechless. Had he meant it when he'd said he was tempted to touch me? I wouldn't mind testing his control. It was the first time a man had admitted he could lose control because of *me*. Not even Sandro showed me such unbridled passion. His kisses were... polite, not filled with unrestrained lust. I hadn't expected a man like Rennie to have any interest in me unless he was taunting me.

"Did you mean what you said?" I asked in the darkness. Only the lights of the ship offered a small amount of illumination.

"You aren't sleeping."

"Answer me."

"No."

Oh, the nerve of the man. "Why not?"

"I don't like where the conversation is going."

"It isn't going anywhere because we aren't having a conversation," I said, propping myself up on my elbows. Even in the semidarkness, I could spot the burning pits of his eyes staring at me.

"Good night, Monia."

"You're impossible." I punched the pillow and lay down, muttering curses that made him chuckle.

I must have dozed off because a rhythmic noise woke me up. Footfalls padded from the silent corridor. A cold shiver crawled up my back, like a file of ants. The light from the passageway limned the door, which meant Rennie wasn't sitting in front of it.

"Rennie?" I whispered.

"Shush," he said, close to me. "Quiet."

Two shadows cut the flow of light on the floor as the footsteps stopped in front of my door. I touched around on my bed, and when I found Rennie's hand, I held it. His big, warm hand closed around mine in a reassuring gesture that slowed my pulse. Until the knob turned. I squeezed Rennie's hand harder. He uncoiled his body as the door inched inwards.

Dread froze me on the spot. A man slid inside, nearly silent on his feet. Judging from his size and build, he was the same man who had attacked Rennie. The moment he stepped forwards, Rennie lunged. A loud thud resounded when they dropped to the floor. I scrambled out of bed and lit the gas lamp on the nightstand with trembling hands. Not that there was much to see. Rennie and the man were entwined together, rolling on the floor. Punches rained on both of them. Thuds, smacks, and kicks made me jolt.

With an animalistic groan, the man shoved Rennie back and darted out of the cabin. Rennie shot after him. The door swung back and forth behind him.

Shaking, I left the quiet corner and tiptoed to the door. I wasn't sure why I was tiptoeing. It seemed pretty useless, but my brain was dealing with an overload of fear the likes of which I'd never experienced before. No, that wasn't true. There had been that time when—pain burst in my head. I rubbed my forehead and squeezed my eyes before peeking into the corridor. What in blazes was happening to me?

There was no one, and aside from a low rumble, the passageway was quiet. I locked the door with trembling hands and searched for my shoes. Rennie had to be safe. He was a strong man. But the other chap was bigger. I could call Detective Norton, though.

There was a knock on the door. "Monia? It's me."

"Rennie." I pulled the door open and without thinking, threw myself over to him.

He caught me in his arms and held me by my waist. The contact with his hard body calmed the brewing storm of fear in my chest. Through the thin fabric of my nightgown, his large palms burned my skin.

"I was so worried," I whispered in the crook of his neck.

"I'm all right." He drew slow circles over my back.

When I stopped quivering, I disentangled myself from him, avoiding gazing at him. "The man?"

"Gone. I tried to keep up with him, but I lost him." A mirthless chuckle left him. "This bloody ship is a maze of ladders and narrow corridors with a lot of steam and loud noises."

I licked my dry lips. "Will the thing you have to do in Cairo help catch that man?"

He gently brushed a lock of my hair from my cheek. "Yes."

"Then I'll do whatever you ask me."

A beam brightened his face. "You should say that more often."

―――――

YES, I'D PROMISED Rennie I would have done everything he said, but as we walked along the pavement of Al-Muizz Street in Cairo, I really wanted to take my time and wander through the beautiful city.

The cobbled street was simply magical, full of colours, singing people, and vendors who sold all sorts of goods, from deliciously smelling food to turquoise pendants. Women in long dresses embroidered with gold and silver strolled around, their silk scarves fluttering behind them. I glanced down at my dark-red skirt with a matching jacket and hat. I envied those women's dresses. They flowed beautifully over the women's legs, showing the tips of their sandalled feet. And the elaborate, stained-glass windows were works of art. I could watch them all day. Not to mention the aristocratic palaces that—

"Don't even think about it," Rennie said.

"Think what?"

"To go around and play tourist. We're here for another reason."

I pouted. "I simply know we're here to do something that is somehow connected to our pursuit of the elusive man who attacked us for some reason. That's quite vague."

"You said you were going to do whatever I asked you to do. So don't wander around."

"But this place is magnificent!" I spread my arms. "So alive and colourful. I'd like to try one of those bowls of rice and lentils, or take a look at that dress shop, and can you smell the bread?"

"Not now." He took my elbow and steered me away from a vendor smiling at me.

It was a good thing Rennie was leading me because I kept getting distracted by the buildings towering over the street and the stone arches soaring above us to watch where we were going. In fact, I was so distracted I didn't notice Rennie ushering me towards a quiet alleyway.

"It's time," he said, searching his pocket.

"For what?" I craned my neck to take a look at the bazaar. "Blazes, is that a camel? I think it's beautiful. Look at the cute muzzle and the way it chews."

"I have to blindfold you." Those few words caused my mood to plummet all the way to China.

"Do you really have to?"

"'Fraid so." He gave me a pointed look. "Please?"

I sighed and mourned the loss of the magnificent colours of Cairo as he wrapped a black cloth around my head.

"You trust me, don't you?" he asked, tying the piece of fabric behind my head.

"Absolutely not," I quipped.

"Excellent." Amusement laced his voice. He took my hand and guided me somewhere.

A bell chimed. We must have entered a shop because cool air hit my cheeks and the scent of thousands of spices teased my nostrils. He exchanged a few words with a man in Arabic.

"Since when do you speak Arabic?" I asked, trying to discreetly touch around.

"I don't speak Arabic. I just know a few sentences, and don't touch anything." He held my probing hand. "There are breakable things here."

"Yes, there are. You're a brute. I'll tell my father how poorly you've treated me."

"Then he'll have me flogged, remember? You don't want that."

"Maybe I do."

He chuckled. "We're going down a flight of stairs. I'd suggest you focus on your steps and think about where you put those pretty feet of yours."

I flushed, glad he wouldn't see my reddened cheeks under the cloth. "Even my feet are pretty?"

"Careful." He laughed. "Everything about you is pretty."

Oh, goodness.

He held my hands while we climbed down and down. The air turned chilly and smelled of moss. Not an ounce of fear or worry coursed through me, though. I did trust him after all. He could be taking me anywhere. No one knew I was there—wherever there was. Anything could happen to me.

My heartbeat remained stable, and my hands didn't sweat. His arm coiled around my waist and pressed me against him. His warmth reached my skin, and my breath hitched.

"Are you scared?" he asked, the amusement gone from his tone. "Is this too much?"

"No."

His fingers sprawled over my waist. "Glad to hear it."

"Did you mean what you said last night?" I asked as he helped me down another flight of stairs.

"Every word." Even in the darkness, I could tell he was watching me. The weight of his stare was like a caress on my skin. His voice sounded low and intense.

"Oh," was all I managed to say.

"Surprised?" he asked, pulling me closer. His breath feathered over my cheek.

"Well, it doesn't happen every day... men usually don't, you know... I'm not such a stunning woman." I was stammering and staggering. Brilliant.

"That's not true." His whispered words rang intimate and personal, causing my breath to come out faster. "But it's true that men can be stupid."

I let out a nervous chuckle.

"And did you mean it?" he asked as we walked along a flat stretch.

"What?"

"When you asked me to touch you, did you mean it? Or was it the green serum?"

I leant against him. "I meant every word."

He growled. "Bugger me."

Maybe it was the darkness that gave the illusion of privacy. Or maybe it was just me, but I put a hand on his chest, stopping him. He didn't ask what I was doing, thank goodness, because I didn't know. I explored the hard wall of his chest until I touched his neck and slid my hand over his nape. Pulse thundering, I pulled him down. He hesitated, but I didn't as I pressed my lips against his. The kiss started a burst of emotions that went through me down to my toes. He cupped my cheek with infinite gentleness and rubbed his thumb over the curve of my jaw while his lips moved over mine. It wasn't like kissing Sandro. The kiss had all the raw intensity Rennie possessed. Not perfect but passionate and wild. It made my body sensitive. I pressed myself against him shamelessly. He caressed my back, waist, and bottom, grazing my lips. I was shivering in his arms, but he withdrew.

"Monia," he whispered. Desperation and pain filled the single word. "I can't."

I licked my bottom lip so I could still taste him. "I know."

He hugged me, pressing me against his body, and tucked my head under his chin. I rested my cheek over his chest right where the pounding of his heart screamed for me.

"We're almost there," he said, brushing his lips over my cheek.

"Let's go." Still leaning against him, I walked along the corridor, then another flight of stairs.

We stopped on flat ground. There must be light shining from somewhere because the air was warmer there than it'd been upstairs. The noise of working hinges rose, then the sound of footsteps and voices hit my ears. I was itching to take a peek, but seemingly reading my mind, Rennie held my hands in his grip.

"Be patient."

I relaxed in his hold. Those hands enveloped mine firmly, but gently, sending a delicious sensation up my legs. A combination of English and Arabic echoed. There were people living underground, and judging by the noise, there were many of them. Rennie exchanged a few more words in Arabic with a man and led me onwards.

"Where are we?" I asked, tilting my head to hear better.

"Sit here. There's a lady who will keep you company." He sat me down.

"A lady?" My rear touched the padding of a soft cushion on the floor. "Are you going to leave me?"

"Not for long." He caressed my jaw with so much tenderness I wanted to moan. "See you later. No pun intended." He laughed, but I sneered at him.

A door closed, and I found myself alone and in the dark. I was about to rip the blindfold from my face when footfalls padded closer.

"Good afternoon," a feminine voice said next to me. "I'm Ife." She spoke perfect English with a lovely, musical lilt I could listen to for hours.

"Hello, Ife." I turned in the general direction of the voice. "I'm Monia."

"Would you like some tea?"

"Yes, please."

There was some shuffling around and the jingling of cups and saucers.

"Here you are. Be careful, it's hot." Ife took my hands and gave me a warm cup.

"Thank you." The scent of cinnamon and jasmine filled the air. I sipped the delicious tea while Ife remained quiet. Taken by a sudden inspiration, I asked, "Is this the Royal Occult Bureau?"

She coughed. "I can't say anything about what this place is. I'm sorry." The words came out too quickly.

Ha! But she'd already answered. Not that her answer gave me any further clue. She could say we were in Buckingham Palace, and it would be the same for me. I tried to remove the blindfold, but Ife stopped me with a gentle hand.

"Please, I'll be in trouble if you remove the blindfold."

Dash it. She said the only thing that would stop me. I didn't want her to be punished because of me. Same old, same old. So I sipped my tea quietly.

At my third cup of tea, the need to visit the lady's room grew, but the door opened, and two pairs of footsteps approached.

"Monia, it's me," Rennie said close to me. "We're going back to the ship."

"Already? But I haven't done anything here." I lowered the cup, hoping not to spill the tea.

"It's all right." He sounded even closer. "We need to leave."

Oddly enough, the sound of his voice rained a sense of calm over me. Although tension was radiating from him.

"Of course."

He took my hands and pulled me up. "A man is here. He'll come on board with us," he whispered.

"Miss Fitzwilliam," a male voice said in English. "I'm Mr Oliver George, and I'll help Rennie catch the man who attacked you."

He kissed my hand. I didn't trust men whose surname was another name because it was jolly confusing.

Rennie's hand replaced Oliver's. "That's enough, Oliver." He folded my hand over his chest where I could feel the steady thump of his heart. "Let's go, shall we?"

NINE

MR OLIVER GEORGE HAD A THIN, long nose that tended to stick into other people's business as I came to learn rather quickly.

After I tried—and failed—to extract information from Rennie about the Royal Occult Bureau and the reason Oliver was with us—was he an expert in catching elusive men on board a ship?—I sat at the dining table with him. Oliver was somewhere on board, investigating, apparently. The information I managed to get from Rennie was always vague.

"Are you going to sleep in my cabin again?" I asked, swallowing a spoonful of pea soup and pretending to be cold and detached.

"Yes." He stared at me from the other side of the table, his tone unapologetic.

I wasn't as shocked or outraged as my mother would like me to be. "Am I still in danger?"

He sucked in a deep breath and put down his fork and knife. "Yes."

But if everyone kept saying I was in danger without telling me from whom or what, how could I protect myself? Right then, a movement from the other side of the room caught my attention. As if summoned by a spell, a vision of Sandro flashed across my mind as he fixed his gaze on me. The scar on my wrist itched, and at the same time, a slash of pain flogged my head. I rubbed my temples.

I saw a long dark corridor. There were no windows. It was suffocating. Anonymous doors lined the passageway. Then blood flickered in my vision, so much blood. My blood. I was bleeding. I was dying. The pain in my arm was burning through me. Mother's desperate face swept into view. She yelled at me not to leave her and implored me to stay with her. But keeping my eyes open was so hard, and the pain was too intense. My mother shook me by the shoulders, screaming my name.

"Monia." Rennie was holding my hand, rubbing my inner wrist with his thumb. His eyebrows were drawn together. "What's the matter? You're so pale."

"I don't know." I rubbed my forehead.

His thumb stroking my skin helped me focus on the present. His touch was soothing and spilt warmth within me. I didn't want him to stop.

"Do you need a doctor?" he asked, peering at my face. "Is it the headache again?"

"Yes. It's killing me." I inhaled deeply. "I need the ladies' room."

"Of course." He rose to his feet.

An emotion I couldn't decipher shadowed his eyes. I hesitated, but he didn't say anything. He went to follow me, but I put a hand on his chest.

"The ladies' room is just around the corner. Please, I need a moment."

He scanned the hall before bowing his head. "Please, be careful."

I slogged around the corner, wondering what the visions meant, when Sandro, in flesh and blood, swept into view as if materialising out of thin air. So he wasn't a product of my imagination.

I froze, ready to scream. "Sandro, what are you doing?" Before I could finish, he swept me off my feet and kissed me hard, his mouth eager and commanding.

But there was something different in his kiss. The sweet excitement that usually shuddered through me was missing. No spark ignited within my chest, and my skin didn't tingle with anticipation. It was like kissing a piece of wood unlike the brief kiss with Rennie, which had caused an explosion of sensations within me.

The spot couldn't be more romantic. The moon was reflected in the dark velvet of the sea, scattering around glittering diamonds of light. Potted plants hid us from prying eyes with their large leaves. But the setting didn't do anything to make me feel better.

I pulled away from him. "Please stop."

"How are you?" he asked, caressing the top of my head.

I stepped back from him. "Sandro, I need to know

more about the danger you're in. We're in. A man broke into my room last night and tried to attack me."

His gaze shifted to the floor. "The ship is going to stop in Venice." He took my shoulders and squeezed them lightly. "Come with me. We can find a safe place to stay before going to my kingdom."

A gasp escaped me. "What are you talking about? Eloping?" My parents would have a seizure. I'd be ruined for life. But that wasn't what made me hesitate. Did I want to go with him? He was the embodiment of my wildest dreams and the life he proposed was what I'd longed for since I was a girl. Adventure, excitement, and travels in the company of a handsome man who adored me. What more could a girl ask for? Still, I didn't want to squeal in happiness and jump around. Besides, Rennie... Rennie would... I didn't know where I was going with that thought, but I didn't want to leave Rennie.

Also, I didn't trust Sandro, although he'd never hurt me. He certainly wasn't the man who had attacked me. I'd never felt in danger with him, and he'd had many occasions to hurt me.

"I'll protect you. I swear it." Sandro's eyes lost their warmth, the warmth that had captivated me, and became cold and calculating. A chill seeped into my bones. I put some distance between Sandro and me.

"I need to think about it." Actually, I didn't, but instinct told me not to anger him.

The smile that stretched his full lips was all predatory, sending a shivering chill down my back. "Of course. Take all the time you want." He kissed my forehead gently before walking away and leaving me confused. But unhurt, admittedly.

As I walked back to the dining hall, I brushed past a table where Mrs Morrison was having dinner with a short, boyish man. She gazed up and shot me a glare of pure hatred before leaning closer to the man and whispering something. He turned towards me, then to her, his cheeks flushing.

"I've never seen that woman before, darling. I swear it," the man said.

"She said she danced with you," Mrs Morrison said.

I slowed my pace. Wait. Was the man Mrs Morrison's husband? Edward?

"Excuse me," I said to the not-so-happy couple. "Mrs Morrison, is this man your husband Edward?"

"Of course he is," she said at the same time he said, "I've never danced with you."

A new headache started to pound in my temples. What in blazes was going on? "You're right. I'm sorry. I think I've made a mistake." Blazes, the man couldn't possibly be mistaken for Edward. If the name of the man I'd danced with was Edward. I flashed a smile and scurried away before Mr and Mrs Morrison could ask me more questions and drag me into their marital problems. I headed to Rennie's table, the room spinning a little.

The scowl on his face softened when he peered at me, standing up. "Do you feel better?"

I massaged my forehead. "Actually, no. I've just met Sandro."

"What?" He scanned the hall. "Where is he? How did he come here?"

"I don't know, and before you ask, no, I didn't help him. His presence surprised me as much as it surprises you."

"It can't be," he muttered through his teeth.

"I just wish to lie down and sleep."

He folded his napkin and took my elbow. "I'll take you to your room."

I let him lead me to my cabin, his arm coiling protectively around my waist. The contact with him felt familiar and comforting. Everyone was lying or keeping secrets from me, and I couldn't understand whom I should trust, but Rennie cared about me. It was something.

Rennie's bag and satchel were lying in a corner in my cabin, a sign he meant to stay here. When his arm released me, a tiny pang of disappointment stung my chest.

"Do you have a screen?" he asked.

"No."

He rubbed the back of his neck. "I'll turn around then and give you some privacy while you change." Facing the wall, he opened his satchel and rummaged through it.

I unbuttoned my shirt and untied my skirt and petticoats. Somehow the fact he could hear the swish of fabric as I undressed and knew what I was doing started an illicit pulse between my legs. I washed using the cold water in the basin and a bar of soap, then I slid into my apparently transparent pink nightgown. While I washed and changed, he didn't pay me the slightest bit of attention, but kept reading a stack of documents, his broad shoulders facing me.

When I was tucked under the quilt, I cleared my throat. "You can look now."

He turned around without glancing at me and checked that the door was locked. "Do you mind if I leave the light on for a while?"

"No, I don't."

He settled himself in his usual spot on the floor with his back to the door and kept reading.

"What are you reading?" I asked, propping myself on my elbows.

"A scientific document." A deep line creased his brow.

"Why does every answer you give me have to be so enigmatic?"

"Because the situation we are in is complicated." He flipped through a page.

"You can't possibly be comfortable on the floor." I didn't like the distance between us.

His head snapped up. "I'm fine where I am, thank you." To his credit, he hadn't complained about back pain after he'd slept on the floor.

"Do you want a pillow?" I asked again.

A boyish smile brightened his face. He didn't look so harsh and menacing with that smile. "Don't worry about me."

"But I do." Reluctantly, I lay down and tried to relax.

The dull ache that had tormented me for days was still humming in my head. Sometimes it flared up, but now it was manageable.

"Monia." Rennie stood next to the bed, hands clenched around a document. "I need to ask you something."

"Of course." I sat up again, careful to keep the blanket around my body. "What is it?"

The boyish air was gone, replaced by his hard warrior face. "The man who attacked us last night. Describe him."

"What?"

"It's important."

I straightened, clenching the quilt. "He was tall, with broad shoulders, dark hair cut short. He had a large, strong neck and big fists. A nightmare if you ask me. I've always been afraid of being attacked by a man so big and strong."

"Bloody hell!" He tossed the papers to the floor and ran his hands through his hair. "It's not what we thought. We were wrong. So bloody wrong. How could I have made such a mistake?"

"What are you talking about?"

Instead of answering me, he leant closer and put his hands on my shoulders, eyes ablaze with... dread? "Describe Edward."

"Rennie, what—"

"Please."

"He's blond, quite elegant, and sophisticated with blue eyes. Handsome, but rather cold."

The colour leached out of his face. "Have you seen him again?"

"Yes." I swallowed the hard lump of guilt in my throat. "Briefly on the deck. I'm sorry I didn't tell you."

"It doesn't matter now. Did he tell you he knows that bloody prince?"

I couldn't suppress a gasp. "How do you know that?"

He released my shoulders, his lips forming a white slash. "Monia, we must go back to England. No, don't ask why," he added quickly as I opened my mouth to protest. "When we're in Venice, we'll leave this damn ship and go back home."

Seething anger flamed my blood. "Why can't you tell me the truth? Do you expect me to follow you like a devoted puppy? I don't understand what's happening. I refuse to do anything you ask unless you give me a good reason."

The sinews on the back of his hands stood out when he tightened his fists. "Believe it or not, if I tell you the truth, you might die. Is that a good enough reason for you?"

"No!" I slammed a hand on the bed, not caring that the blanket was slipping down, revealing my flimsy nightgown. "How can knowing the truth be harmful? I believe it's the opposite. How can I protect myself if I don't know the truth?"

"Can't you just trust me?" There was a note of hurt in his voice, which I promptly ignored.

I wasn't going to feel guilty for wanting to know who was attacking me. "I do trust you, but we never talk. You often give me orders and never answer my questions. It's frustrating."

"Fine." He rolled up the sleeves of his shirt and sat on the edge of the bed, causing it to dip. "Let's talk. What do you want to know?"

I hadn't expected that. Squirming on the spot, I wrapped the blooming blanket tighter around me and racked my brain for a question to ask. After a few moments of silence, I asked, "Do you have siblings?"

His fierce expression softened. "An older sister, one year my senior. A pain in the... neck if you ask me. She always said I should write to Mum and visit my niece more often." It was hard to imagine Rennie playing with a little girl.

"Why don't you do it?" I asked, curious.

He shrugged. "Too much work. Laziness. Excuses." He chuckled. "Too many sticky kisses from my niece."

Something melted in my chest at his chuckle. It held enough love to thaw a glacier. "You adore that girl."

A light flush crept up his cheeks, and he looked simply adorable. "She's special, and I'm not saying that because she's my niece. When I take her out for a walk in the country, she always wants to know the names of the flowers and insects. Sometimes I know the answer, but other times, I just make up a funny name to see her smile. The problem is that she has an excellent memory. She notices when I give the same flower two different, made-up names while I don't keep track of them. She becomes so angry on those occasions." He laughed again, and I liked the sound. It was deep and rich and bursting with love. "As a result, she loves checking every fact I tell her. She devours books and tells me all about them. She's so clever. I'm teaching her to carve wood. She's a fast learner."

"I guess she doesn't trust you?" I quipped.

"Good point." He laughed. "I prefer talking to her and playing with her tea set to being around some adults. I feel happy just hearing her laugh."

His love for his niece made my heart flutter. "How did you get this scar?" I traced my fingertip over the pale scar running along his jaw.

He took a sharp intake of breath that did something to my insides. "It happened during a mission."

I didn't ask what he meant by mission not to interrupt him. Besides, I guessed *I* was a mission to him.

"I was chasing a criminal through a maze of alleyways. I got distracted for a moment, and the thug lashed out at me. I managed to jump out of his reach, but I wasn't fast enough. He slashed me." He tilted his head to show me the full extent of the cut.

The scar ran along the column of his neck and disappeared underneath the collar of his shirt.

"Good gracious, he could have killed you." I couldn't resist and traced the whole scar down to the starched collar, feeling his surprisingly smooth skin and the tension underneath it. "The stab. You healed so quickly from it. How?"

"I can't tell you." His chest heaved as he inhaled.

I stroked his neck and chest again. Touching him was mesmerising.

His eyes darkened. "Monia." There was the same desperate need ringing in my name as that time in Cairo. He swallowed hard.

"What do you feel now?" I asked, leaving my hand on his chest.

"It's better if I don't tell you." He regarded me from underneath his long eyelashes.

"No more secrets. Tell me how you feel."

He shook his head. "What if I show you, instead?"

He inched closer. The air between us was charged so much that my skin tingled with anticipation. All my blood flew towards my lips and south. The closer he came, the more heat spread from my core. Kissing him in the dark was one thing. But watching him get closer, his chest swelling and his eyes darkening with desire, was quite another. His lips were a breath away from mine. His body's heat seeped into me, enveloped me, and protected me.

Rennie stopped right when his lips brushed against mine. It was a light touch that sent a shiver up my spine. I parted my lips, and the tip of his tongue darted out. I moaned shamelessly. I clutched his face and held it as his scent filled the air I breathed. Something cracked within me, an explosion of maddening need and passion I'd never experienced. He must have felt it too because he leant into the kiss and bit my lips before running his tongue over them. I opened my mouth, inviting him deeper, but he paused, breathing hard. He touched his forehead to mine.

"I can't," he whispered, pulling away from me.

"But..." I didn't know what to add.

"Your father is going to kill me." He laughed without humour. "Literally."

"He doesn't need to know."

"I gave my word." He caressed my cheek, and I leant against his comforting hand. "It means the world to me. He trusts me, and I don't want to disappoint him, much less lie to him."

Dash it. "I respect that."

Without looking at me, he rose and returned to his cold spot on the floor.

We hadn't decided what to do once we arrived in Venice, but the turmoil of emotions within me was too strong for me to talk to him now. So I lay down and stared at the ceiling, my pulse beating in my ears. My body hadn't reacted like that when Sandro had kissed me. Rennie nearly kissed me and I was ablaze with desire. What was happening?

TEN

THE BLUE EXPANSE of the Mediterranean Sea surrounded us the next day. My knowledge of the sea was limited, but I had a feeling the water here was a lighter shade of blue than the ocean. The warm air was a pleasant change from the vast coldness of the Atlantic.

Another not-so-pleasant change was having two brooding men, Oliver and Rennie, keep such a close eye on me. From breakfast to my afternoon tea, they were always a few feet from me, scanning the room, searching the corridors, and being stiff. When I went to the ladies' room, they would wait for me in the corridor, knocking on the door if the affair required more than two minutes.

As I promenaded along the main deck, enjoying the sunshine, they followed, talking between themselves in hushed tones. They had the same attitude, the same walk, and the same grey suits. Co-workers, obviously.

I couldn't hear what they were saying, but judging by how their fists clenched and their necks tensed, they were arguing. I twirled my parasol, pretending to stare at the horizon while throwing glances at them.

Rennie had been quite distant since the previous night. I couldn't blame him. The contract was clear. No romantic involvement with me. But blazes, if he'd kissed me—properly, that is—I would have let him. If he'd wanted to touch me, I would have allowed it. Oddly enough, not a trace of guilt soured my mouth. Sandro wasn't my betrothed, but I shouldn't be so eager to kiss another man, should I? Or rather, so sad because another man hadn't kissed me.

Still, did I want to return to England? Maybe. The trip was proving to be emotionally confusing and rather dangerous.

"It's her!" a shrieking feminine voice bellowed from behind me. "That woman!"

I turned around to find Mrs Morrison glowering at me. Detective Norton stood next to her, his rounded glasses askew on his nose.

"It's her. She did something to my husband." The woman strode towards me, her dark hair escaping from her tight bun.

Rennie stepped in front of me, blocking my view of the termagant.

She came to an abrupt halt. "What have you done to him, you witch?"

I touched my chest. "Are you talking to me?" I glanced around to be sure she wasn't addressing someone else.

"What's happening here?" Oliver asked, sounding like an affronted British general.

Norton pushed his glasses up and dabbed his forehead with a handkerchief. "Mr Edward Morrison, the husband of Mrs Morrison here, is missing."

"Oh, my goodness," I said. Not another one.

Rennie stiffened. "Since when is he missing?"

"Last night," Mrs Morrison answered. "We went to bed, then he woke up saying he felt sick and that he was going to find the nurse. He never came back, and the nurse didn't see him."

"I'm sorry about your husband," I said. "But I don't have anything to do with his disappearance."

"Did he leave my cabin to meet you?" She jabbed a finger at me. "Did he have an assignation with you?"

"How dare you accuse me of that." I snapped my parasol shut.

Rennie stretched out his arms, as if to keep Mrs Morrison and me separated. "We'll help search for him. You have my word."

"You better find him, or else I'll deal with that scandalous woman myself." She pivoted and marched away.

Scandalous? Me? How exciting!

Norton fiddled with his glasses again. "Miss Fitzwilliam, I must ask you if you have any relationship with Mrs Morrison."

Oh, confound it. Curse Edward. "No. I only saw the man once very briefly. We've never spoken."

Norton showed the sceptical expression only police

officers could master. "But Mrs Morrison said you told her that you and Edward danced together."

Bother. "I was mistaken. The man I danced with was called Edward, but he wasn't Mr Morrison. It was another Morrison. I mean another Edward." It sounded weak to my own ears.

Norton didn't look impressed. "A member of the staff remembers you asking her to find the cabin of Mr Edward Morrison. You were quite insistent on finding him."

Tarnation. Even Rennie cocked his head towards me. Oliver scrubbed his chin.

I hadn't told Rennie. "I, yes, I did, but, see, the man I danced with claimed to be Edward Morrison," I said, tormenting the pommel of my parasol. "But he wasn't."

"Why would anyone pretend to be him?" Norton asked, scribbling something on his notepad.

"I don't know, Detective. I believe finding the answer to that question is your job." I lifted my chin.

He glowered. "And where's this man? The man you danced with?" he pressed on.

"I don't know," I said through gritted teeth. "I haven't seen him recently."

The detective opened his mouth again, but Rennie cut him off. "Shouldn't we focus on the real Mr Morrison and try to find him?"

"But the man Miss Fitzwilliam met might be behind Mr Morrison's disappearance, and who knows, perhaps even Mrs Francis's disappearance." Norton cast a hard glance at me.

Unfortunately, he had a point, but I didn't want to answer any of his questions.

"Let's search the ship first. We have some experience with it now." Rennie took my arm and led me away without giving Norton the chance to answer. "Why didn't you tell me you searched for Edward?" he asked when we were out of earshot.

"I didn't think it was important, and since you didn't give me any information about the danger I was in, I wasn't sure Edward had anything to do with it. I'm not sure even now. Dash it, I'm confused."

He glared at me, the warmth from last night gone. "Listen, I promise I'll tell you everything I can, everything that doesn't harm you. Is there anything else you didn't tell me?" I must have looked guilty because his expression hardened. "What is it?"

"Sandro wants to elope with me once we're in Venice," I whispered.

Not a single hint of shock or surprise showed on his face. Sort of disappointing. I was expecting a bigger reaction.

"Did you agree?" His tone was inquisitive but not jealous.

"I didn't, of course. What a ridiculous idea. I don't lose my head only because a man is a good kisser."

His nostrils flared a bit. "Let's find this bloody Morrison." He added three 's' in Morrison.

We didn't split. Rennie and Oliver went everywhere I went, from the restaurant on the top-level deck to the sauna. It was dusk when we searched the theatre. No silver goo stained the floor, though.

I plonked down onto one of the plush seats, heaving a sigh. "Norton will accuse me of murder."

Oliver shrugged. "No body, no crime."

"We need an entire unit to search this bloody ship," Rennie muttered, running a hand through his hair.

"An entire unit of what?" I asked, perking up.

He worked his jaw. "I have to talk with Norton. Oliver, take care of Monia." With that, he strode away.

Oliver offered me his arm. "I'll escort you to dinner, Miss Fitzwilliam."

We walked towards the dining hall, him humming a tune, me wishing Rennie were the one with me. Without much appetite, I picked at my baked trout, searching the dining hall for Rennie. He'd been gone for a while. At least he was going to sleep in my cabin tonight. We would talk.

"Worried, Miss Fitzwilliam?" Oliver asked, smiling politely while drinking his tea with his little finger stretched out.

"I wonder where Rennie might be."

He tilted his head. "Am I not a good company?"

"No." The word rushed out of my mouth. Good gracious, since when was I so rude? My face flamed. "I'm sorry. I didn't mean that."

He sipped his tea. "May I ask how you got that scar?" He pointed at my wrist.

I hadn't noticed my sleeve had inched up, revealing a

portion of the long scar. "An incident while I was riding my horse."

He edged closer, a wicked glint in his eyes. "Are you sure about that? Are you sure it isn't something else? Something more sinister?"

As he said those words, a headache pounded behind my eyes and cold sweat dampened my skin. "Of course I am." My reply lacked confidence. My memories were confused. There wasn't a horse. I winced as pain sliced through me.

He smirked and leant back on the chair. "Interesting."

I cheered up when Rennie entered the room, his face a mask of frustration.

"We found Mr Morrison," he said.

"Lord, is he all right?" I asked, standing up.

"He's weak, but alive." Rennie pinched the bridge of his nose. "We found him in the cargo hold, still wearing his dressing gown. He's now with the nurse."

"Good. Now he'll tell Norton I have nothing to do with this business," I said, pushing aside my plate.

Rennie shook his head. "Monia, he said you attacked him."

"What?" The little amount of dinner I'd eaten churned in my stomach. "This is absurd. I've never touched him."

"I believe you, but Norton wants to see you." Rennie offered me his crooked arm. "Now."

"I'll go see Morrison," Oliver said. "See you later."

On weak legs, I headed to Norton's office, holding Rennie's arm. "Can he arrest me?"

"That's not going to happen. Ever. I won't allow it." He patted my hand.

"But what if he wants to?"

"No." The certainty in his tone brought some hope to my chest.

"Miss Fitzwilliam." Norton stood up from his chair when we entered his office. "Please take a seat."

I did as told and perched on the wooden chair in front of the desk. Rennie stood next to me, towering over the detective.

"Mr Steele must've told you we found Mr Morrison." Norton laced his fingers over the desk.

I didn't say anything, waiting for a question.

"Mr Morrison said you lured him to the cargo hold with an excuse and then you... er, threw yourself at him and ravished him." The detective shifted on his chair. His forehead glistened with sweat. "He said you started kissing him and doing other illicit things, trying to seduce him."

My mouth dropped open. "He must be out of his mind, or perhaps he hit his head somewhere. I did no such thing. I have no romantic interest in him."

"Besides." Rennie chewed on his bottom lip. "Miss Fitzwilliam didn't leave her cabin last night."

Norton squirmed, as if his chair were on fire. "May I ask you how you know that?"

My reputation was ruined either way. But I'd rather ruin my good name by telling the truth than be arrested for a lie. "Rennie slept in my cabin." I didn't care how it sounded. "We've been together all the time."

"I see." Norton drummed his fingers on the table.

"Detective." Rennie's grave tone filled the room. "I wouldn't put Miss Fitzwilliam's reputation in jeopardy for no reason. What we told you is the truth. Miss Fitzwilliam didn't leave her cabin last night."

"I understand but"—Norton dropped the pencil he was writing with—"why would Mr Morrison lie? Why would he accuse Miss Fitzwilliam without reason? Revenge? He doesn't know her."

"Maybe he was confused," I said. "Maybe he met someone who looked like me, who pretended to be me." Yes, it sounded far-fetched.

Norton's chair made a squeaky noise when he reclined in it. "So we have a man who pretended to be Mr Morrison and who danced with you, and now a woman who pretended to be you and attacked the real Mr Morrison. Not to mention that Mrs Francis vanished after claiming to have been attacked by a phantom Scot no one has ever seen. A quite complicated web that involves a lot of people."

Summarised like that, it sounded absurd. And it was. But I had no answers.

"Detective," I said, on the verge of a hysterical breakdown. "Believe me. I did not hurt Mr Morrison. I don't know what's happening on this ship, but I am not a criminal. Or a seductress." My eyes burned with tears, and I hoped Norton didn't think I was faking them.

He sagged on the chair. "I'll interrogate Mr Morrison

again when he feels better. You can go for now, Miss Fitzwilliam."

I didn't like the 'for now,' but I bowed my head and stood up.

"This is preposterous," I said when we were in the corridor, heading to my cabin. "You don't believe I attacked Morrison, do you?"

"Of course not." He put a hand on the small of my back. "Don't worry. No one is going to arrest you."

I snuggled closer to him, resting my head on his shoulder before straightening back up. Oliver was leaning against the wall next to my door.

"Did you speak with Morrison?" I asked.

He shook his head. "He was asleep. He's very weak." He glanced at Rennie. "As if he hadn't slept or eaten for days. His energy drained."

"What did the attacker do to him? Why is he so weak?" I opened the door of my cabin with a shaky hand.

"It's complicated." Oliver slid inside the cabin while Rennie remained in the corridor.

"What's happening?" An anxious knot tightened in my belly.

"Oliver will keep an eye on you tonight." Rennie's voice sounded all wrong, as if he were angry.

"Rennie needs to sleep too," Oliver said, starting to shut the door.

"I..." I fiddled with my hands.

"Good night, Rennie." Oliver waved.

"Be a gentleman, Oliver," Rennie hissed.

Oliver smirked. "You have my word."

Rennie held up a hand. "Good night, Monia."

"But I'd like you to stay here," I said.

Oliver stepped in front of me. "Rennie is exhausted. He didn't sleep to keep guard. He'll be with you tomorrow."

Indeed, dark shadows circled Rennie's eyes. "I'll stay with you tomorrow," he said.

"Good night." I wanted to say something else, but Oliver locked the door.

"Now." He removed his jacket and tossed it over a chair. "Don't worry, Miss Fitzwilliam. I'll be the perfect gentleman, even though I'm not good company."

"Perhaps Rennie could sleep here too." I balled my fists at my hips.

He waited a few moments, then peeked outside. "Good. He's gone. We need to have a chat."

"About what?" I stepped away from him.

"Rennie and I disagree. See, I believe sacrifices must be made for a good cause." He flexed his fingers.

"I don't understand." I inched closer to the vase on the dresser. It was heavy enough to cause some damage in case he attacked me.

"Do you want to know why your parents sent you away with Rennie? Why didn't they like your prince? Why did a man try to attack you? Who really is Edward? And why does Morrison claim you attacked him?" He had my attention now.

"I do," I said, still touching the vase.

"I can help you with that." He put his hand on my forehead, and I jolted. "Relax, Monia. This is going to sting a little."

Pain burst inside me. White flashes filled my vision. Fire seemed to flow through my lungs. It was as if a red-hot blade were cutting my head in two. I screamed, my throat hurting. Then darkness enveloped me.

ELEVEN

PEOPLE WERE ARGUING AROUND ME. Men. They shouted, but one of them shouted louder than anyone else. He sounded furious, almost murderous. He sounded like Rennie.

My head hurt so much that I didn't have the energy to tell them to be quiet. I couldn't understand what they were saying. Nausea was roiling my stomach. I couldn't open my eyes. If I opened them, I was sure I would die from the pain. So I drifted back into sleep.

Strange dreams flashed across my mind. But somehow, I knew they weren't dreams. They were memories. Things I'd forgotten. I was trekking along a path in the Dolomites. Yes, I'd been used to travelling with my parents. They'd taken me everywhere with them. No restrictions. No rules. Only freedom. We didn't see touristic places, though, but remote locations with poisonous plants, wild creatures, and spiders bigger than my hand. I loved it. Travelling with them and seeing new places always excited me and made me happy.

It was a sunny day, one of those rare days when not a cloud darkened the sky. We'd been hiking up and down mountains for weeks. Mother was walking next to me. Father brought up the rear.

My parents were chasing a creature, an Unnatural, a beast that had attacked a few climbers, but they weren't sure what the creature was. Both my father and mother were occult agents for the Royal Occult Bureau. It was their job to capture Unnaturals who killed humans, from vampires to ghosts and witches. I was learning how to be an agent during our trips together. I learnt things they wouldn't teach me at a normal school. We paused in front of a panoramic view. The breeze carried the scent of flowers and wet grass. But Father was nervous, always searching the shadows. His hand twitched over the grip of his gun.

"It's so beautiful," I said, dabbing my sweaty forehead with a handkerchief.

"Listen," Father said, "I'll take you back to the hotel, and your mother and I will search this part of the forest for the Unnatural. I think it's going to be too dangerous for you."

"Nonsense." Mother rolled her eyes. "Monia is strong and clever enough to stay with us."

"Laura." The slant of Father's lips showed his displeasure. "What we taught her isn't enough. We've been searching for this creature for days. It's clever, elusive, and I'm worried. There's a strange smell in the air."

I cleared my throat, not liking that they were talking about me as if I weren't there. "May I say something?"

Both of them whipped their heads towards me, matching frowns on their faces.

"I wish to stay with you," I said, tugging at the straps of my rucksack. "Perhaps the creature isn't clever or elusive. It simply isn't here. This place is too beautiful to spend the day in a hotel room, and I can take care of myself." Those proved to be my last famous words. I spun around to face the forest and started up the path. It winded through white spruce trees and tall birches that formed a green tunnel around me.

"... she isn't a child," Mother said.

"She needs to learn how to fight an Unnatural." Father had a point, but in the few years during which I followed my parents, nothing had ever happened.

As I stepped into the shadows, the cold seeped into me. Behind me, my parents kept arguing in hushed tones. A sense of oppression choked me, and I paused to loosen the collar of my shirt. The moment I put a hand on a tree bank to rest, an animal that looked like an eel came out of the ground. Its sharp teeth dribbled with drool. The long, sleek body coiled around me, shutting up my scream. My ribs cracked. A burning pain struck my wrist when the beast closed its toothy mouth around it. My entire arm was burning. My bones were breaking. I couldn't breathe.

Father and Mother wrestled against the beast, punching, stabbing, and kicking it, but the pain blinded me, and I couldn't see clearly what was happening. The monster's powerful grip loosened until sweet air rushed back into my lungs. I fell to the ground, my body limp and sore.

"Monia." Mother took my face, her features contorted by worry and tears clinging to her lashes. "You'll be all right."

But I wasn't all right. I was broken, scared, and scarred for life.

Even after my body healed from the wounds, my mind wouldn't. The attack had ruined me. I couldn't sleep. I couldn't eat. I didn't want to leave the house. I didn't want to travel with my parents. I didn't want to be an occult agent any longer. I didn't want to see anyone.

That was when my parents told me that an occult agent could remove the bad memories, make me forget, so I'd get better. At first, I wasn't sure. Forgetting everything sounded good, but what if the fear lingered? I wanted to be normal again.

Besides, recovering the memories was possible but extremely dangerous. My mind could be permanently damaged. My heart might stop from the stress and pain.

But I wanted to stop the nightmares and the constant, all-consuming fear of being attacked. Tired and in pain, I agreed to be cleansed. Every trace of the Royal Occult Bureau and the Unnaturals was deleted from my mind.

After the cleansing, I started to live again. The fear disappeared with the memories.

My parents kept me in the house as much as possible,

worried about me. All those years I'd blamed them for doing what I'd told them to do. I'd agreed to have my memories removed. It'd been my choice, and I understood why my parents were overprotective. Guilt was a bitter taste burning the back of my mouth. A lump swelled in my throat. Hurt, remorse, and shame formed a powerful combination.

Oliver and Rennie were occult agents. Their grey suits and strong bodies gave them away. Oliver had forced my memories to surface again. Now I understood why my parents had sent me away. Sandro was an Unnatural, but I couldn't tell which species. My knowledge was limited. They'd sent me away because they were worried I might be hurt again or remember everything if I became too close to Sandro. Rennie had been right. He couldn't tell me anything. If he had, he would have risked causing my memories to resurface, hurting me, and destroying my brain.

But I remembered now. Everything.

I opened my eyes, panting. The room was quiet, no loud voices. Every inch of my body was in pain, and the light from the gas lamps hurt my eyes. But I wasn't in my cabin. The room was too wide. It had a soaring ceiling with frescoes of flowers and animals. Little roses were painted on the wall, crawling up towards the domed ceiling. Where was I? I sat up, waiting for my head to stop spinning. The white nightgown I was wearing had long sleeves that covered my bandaged hands. Even my leg was bandaged. I flexed my fingers. Pain shot up my arms.

After putting my feet on the marble floor, I tried to stand up. When my legs didn't tremble, I took a slow step towards the diamond window, walking past a polished nightstand and dresser. My unbridled hair fell in waves to my waist as I slogged onwards.

There wasn't a cobbled street below the window, but a narrow canal where murky water flowed. The opposing building was so close I could touch it if I stretched out my arm. Narrow tripartite windows, decorated with complicated motifs, opened to the view. There was only one city so beautiful. Venice. The SS *Florentia* had arrived in Venice. Where was Rennie?

I slid on a dressing gown that lay at the foot of the bed and left the bedroom. "Is anyone here?" My voice sounded coarse. So I cleared my throat and said again, "Hello?"

Everything was narrow here, even the corridor. A door was flung open. My heart gave a thump of anticipation before taking a dip to my stomach. It was Detective Norton. His eyes widened when he spotted me.

"Miss Fitzwilliam, how are you?" he asked, hurrying towards me.

"Spectacular. Where's Rennie?" I put a hand on the wall not to fall.

"It's complicated." He adjusted his glasses.

All the blood flowed down from my head. "What happened to him?"

"Why don't you sit down?" He took my elbow and led me back to the bedroom. "We are in a hospital of sorts. A small practice that offers rooms to the patients as well."

"Fascinating. Where's Rennie?" I was growing tired of asking the same question.

The detective didn't speak until I was sitting on a stuffed chair and—if I'd been more relaxed—I would have appreciated how soft and silky it was.

"You've been sick for days." He started. "The doctor on board the *Florentia* didn't know what to do. So we had to disembark you here in Venice. Rennie and his friend Oliver had a furious brawl. They came to blows. Then Rennie sent a wire to your parents—"

"Oh, no!" I clamped my hands over my mouth. "What did they do to him?"

He opened his mouth, but the door was pushed inwards, and my mother rushed inside. Her face, so similar to mine, was stricken with grief. Lack of sleep clouded her dark eyes.

"Monia." She held me in a tight embrace, caressing the top of my head. "I left your side for a moment, and you woke up."

"Mother." I clung to her with all my strength and wept on her shoulder.

She didn't say anything but let me cry while stroking my head.

When Mother wiped my tears with her handkerchief, Norton wasn't in the room. I hadn't heard him leave.

"We were so worried." She took my face and studied it, peering into my eyes with clinical interest. "You could have died."

"Mama." I took her hands. As much as I was happy to

see her, I needed to know Rennie was safe. "Where's Rennie?"

Her face straightened. "He knew the consequences of putting you in danger."

"It wasn't him." Pain burst within me as I raised my voice. "It was Oliver who unlocked my memories. Rennie tried to protect me. Mama, please don't tell me he was hurt."

"He's with your father. Here in Venice, there's an occult department called the Demonic Unit. Rennie is in a cell there, waiting to be judged."

"Mother!" I thumped a fist on the armchair, sending a fresh shot of pain up my arm. "He didn't do anything. I demand to see him. Immediately."

"You need rest." She gave me the stern look she always wore when I was about to disobey. "The process of making your memories resurface caused your skin to burn, and your body to weaken. It needs time to recover."

"Sod the rest."

A gasp left her as she stepped away from me. "Monia! Manners."

I folded my arms over my chest, sending a fresh shot of pain up my arms. "I want to see Rennie. Now."

VENICE WAS INDEED the most elegant and beautiful city in Europe. I could easily believe it. The architecture was stunning with all those palaces, balconies, and cathedrals that looked like wedding cakes. But holy smoke, the smell wasn't impressive. Some canals smelled of mould. Others filled the air with heavy humidity that hung on my hair and skin. Thank goodness the sea breeze refreshed the alleyways.

The knot of worry in my belly didn't ease when Mother and I entered St Mark's Basilica. The church was truly stunning. The gable shone with blue enamel and was dotted with golden stars. The inside was an explosion of light with rays of sunshine flooding in from the windows and the soaring ceiling. It was like being engulfed in sunlight and colours.

"Is Rennie here?" I asked, admiring the frescoes.

"This is the entrance to the Venetian Demonic Unit. There aren't many underground tunnels here, obviously. The Demonic Unit stretches on the rooftops, and every church allows you to enter it."

We crossed the nave, and Mother headed for an anonymous wooden door in a nook. A flight of stairs started leading up. I might have overestimated my strength because I was wheezing after two minutes of going up. The skin on my hands and feet burned, causing me to wince at each step.

"Do you want to rest?" Mother asked. She wasn't even breathing hard. But then again, she'd been an occult agent for nearly twenty years. Her brows drew together as she regarded me with concern and so much love it warmed my chest.

"No, I want to see Rennie."

She exhaled, shaking her head.

With new determination, I resumed going up. We arrived at a landing where a window offered a spectacular view of the Venetian Lagoon and the city's canals. I could get used to a view like that, compared to the dark underground tunnels of the Royal Occult Bureau in Oxford. The long corridor lined with doors was a more familiar sight.

Gentlemen and ladies in blue velvet uniforms walked along the corridor, casting polite glances at us. I craned my neck to take a better look at their outfits. Blazes. They were so much better than the dull grey uniforms of the Royal Occult Bureau. Mother took a corridor on the right, then another on the left, then another... I lost count of the turns. Why were the occult bureaus so complicated? After a few minutes of walking, we entered an area with thick stone walls and marble floors.

"It's here." Mother stopped in front of a door reinforced with iron bars. She knocked. "Ernest, it's me."

The door swung inwards, and Father swept into view. His long beard and sagging eyes spoke of sleepless nights and worry that came from the heart.

"Darling." He hugged me fiercely, muttering that he loved me. He shivered, a sob leaving him. "I was so worried."

"Oh, Papa." I inhaled the familiar scent of verbena and tobacco coming from his grey suit.

He patted my back before releasing me. "It shouldn't have happened like that." Tears glistened in his brown eyes.

Mother scoffed. "There is no need to become sentimental, darling. Monia is fine, as you can see."

"Yes, yes." He wiped his eyes with a handkerchief. "My little Monia."

Not so little, but anyway. "It's all right, Papa. I survived." With a lot of pain and blood, but I survived. I swallowed the lump in my throat. Later, I would be more than happy to talk with them about my lost and recovered memories, but for now, I only wanted to see Rennie. "Where's Rennie?"

"Everything for you, sweetheart. Follow me," Father said, a hand on my shoulder.

Using a brass key, he opened yet another door. A breath was punched out of me when I saw Rennie. He was sitting on a wooden bench in a small room with bars on the windows. He was staring at the floor with his shoulders hunched and elbows propped on his knees. A plate of bread, cheese, and fresh fruits lay untouched next to him.

"Rennie." The word came out strangled.

He bolted upright, revealing the cuts and bruises covering him. "Monia."

I rushed towards him and wrapped my arms around him. Dry blood soaked his shirt. One eye was swollen shut, and a cut on his lip showed a thick crust.

"You're all right," he whispered, burying his face in the crook of my neck. "Not seeing you was killing me."

"What have they done to you?" Anger burned in my chest. Had my parents done that to him? I glanced at them.

Mother pursed her lips in a silent challenge, and a flush reddened my father's cheeks.

"It was Oliver." Rennie grinned, releasing me and stepping back. "When I realised what he'd done, I told him I was going to denounce him to the bureau for misconduct. He wasn't too happy."

"Where's Oliver?" The scoundrel.

He caressed my cheek gently. "I don't know. I lost sight of him when we docked in Venice, and I was too worried about you to care about him. But your parents told me the bureau is taking care of him and considering his conduct."

"I hope they give him the sack." Holding his hand, I turned towards my parents. "Papa, you must release him. I'm all right now, and what happened wasn't Rennie's fault."

"Can we talk to you for a moment?" Father held the door open and beckoned me to follow him.

"But—"

"Go, don't worry," Rennie said. He laced his fingers through mine for a moment, eyes filling with happiness, before releasing my hand.

An ache pounded in my chest as I stared at him. At that moment, watching him bruised and defeated because of me, I realised one thing: I'd do anything for him. I wanted to help him and take care of him as he took care of me. Images of him smiling and watching me flashed through my mind. I felt safe and loved when I was with him. How was it possible I'd considered him brusque and harsh? There was nothing harsh about him. Could he tell my feelings had changed? Could he sense my affection for him warming my whole body? Before I ran to him and kissed him, I lowered my gaze not to stare into his shining eyes.

Our fingers remained brushing against each other until the distance between us became too great. But his warmth lingered on my skin. And in my heart.

TWELVE

FATHER SHOWED ME to a parlour with a blue silk sofa and matching armchairs. I'd been to the Royal Occult Bureau in Oxford a few times, but I hadn't seen such lovely furniture. The bureau didn't spend a lot of money on comfortable armchairs and silk wallpaper. Still, the lovely room did nothing to ease the knot of worry in my belly. I sat on the armchair in front of my parents, feeling like a witness at a trial.

"When can Rennie leave the cell?" I asked.

Father plopped onto the sofa and sighed. "Rennie signed a contract."

"The contract is poppycock," I said, earning a glare from Mother. "He did nothing but protect me. Oliver wronged me." The return of my memories was more than welcome though. The fear of being attacked and the pain of that day were still vivid in my mind, but at least I was aware of who Sandro was. He'd charmed me, and I'd fallen for his tricks only because I'd lost my memories. And he'd developed an obsession with me and was chasing me. Not that I could blame my parents or anyone else.

"We trusted Rennie. He has an impeccable record. The agents at the bureau talk highly of him. But we don't know him well," Mother said in an icy tone. "We couldn't choose someone you were familiar with not to trigger your memories. The contract was the only protection we could give you." Her lips flattened in a white slash. "You seem rather fond of him."

"And he of you," Father said, smiling.

"We're only friends." My answer came out in a rush of words that tripped over each other. "There's nothing romantic between us." I wasn't sure if I was saying that because it was true or because I wanted to protect Rennie from being flogged. "I care for him very much. He's been nothing but kind to me. Please I need to be with him."

A strained silence fell after my last words. I didn't sound like a woman trying to protect a friend.

"Darling." Mother touched my hand. "He isn't the man we wish to see you with. He's an ordinary occult agent with an average salary. Not to mention the constant threat of being killed by one of the Unnaturals he encounters daily."

"He isn't so ordinary." My tone was defensive. Mother's words were scrubbing me like sand. "And I wouldn't care about his position or salary... if I were interested in him, that is." Father opened his mouth, but in a bold move that didn't belong to me, I cut him off. "All I'm asking you is not to hurt him. There's no need for that. He didn't breach any rules."

"He put you in danger," Mother said in a low voice.

"But Oliver—"

"Forget Oliver! He didn't sign a contract with us. It was Rennie's duty to take care of you, and he failed." Mother rose. "Yes, Oliver has his faults, and so has Rennie. The *Florentia* is still moored at the port of Venice. We will retrieve your luggage and then return home, and that's it."

I remained still for a few moments. "No," I said.

"Excuse me?" Mother tilted her head.

Father fiddled with his hands.

"I said no." I stood up as well. "First, I'm not a child. I can make my own decisions, and I've decided to stay."

"For what reason?" Mother asked, shock widening her eyes.

"I don't want to run from an Unnatural. Now that my memories are back, I want to face my fear. I want to face this Unnatural who's chasing me." The confidence filling me now would be gone in half an hour, when I realised what I was getting myself into, but I meant what I said. "And I want Rennie to help me. We've started this trip together. We're going to finish it together on board the SS *Florentia*. We paid for the whole trip."

Father shook his head. "It's too dangerous. You're coming back home with us."

"No," I repeated, and it was liberating. "I don't want to hide. I want to do something instead of fleeing, or I will flee for the rest of my life."

Tension charged the air. It was the first time I'd challenged my parents. I'd always been obedient and meek, and I ended up being chased by an Unnatural and completely helpless. Not anymore.

"You want to bait the Unnatural to catch him." My mother's lips thinned. "This is too dangerous."

"Sandro is hunting me. It's time for me to become the hunter and him the prey. I would appreciate it if you freed Rennie from his cell." I tilted my chin up. "We have a ship to board and an Unnatural to catch."

I HADN'T EXPECTED my parents to agree to my decision so quickly. I must have been jolly convincing because ten minutes after my outburst, I was in a gondola, heading for the port, and Rennie was sitting next to me. They'd insisted on meeting me again in Ibiza though, a non-negotiable clause. Rennie was covered in cuts and bruises, but the shot of green serum he'd injected himself with was helping him heal. Because that was what the green serum did. It gave supernatural strength to the occult agents and healed them at uncanny speed, which explained how Rennie had healed so quickly from the stab. A doctor of the Demonic Unit had given me a shot as well, a small dose, just to help with the pain and burns. My skin was nearly normal now.

In the cramped space of the gondola, I couldn't take

my eyes off him. He was so close to me I could touch his thigh when I stretched out a finger.

"How did you convince your parents to let you continue the cruise?" he asked, staring at me with wide eyes.

I withdrew my finger. "I simply told them the truth, that I didn't want to run." I shifted in the seat as the gondola sailed in the canal. "But to be honest, I have no idea how to catch Sandro. I don't even know what kind of Unnatural he is."

"I have an idea, and it's not a pretty one." His knee brushed against mine when the gondola rocked right and left, and my stomach gave a flip. I gazed up, and he licked his lips before resuming talking. "Your parents thought he was an incubus. That's why they sent you away. But the fact he followed you bothered me. Incubi can develop an attachment to their prey but not so quickly. Not without..." He raised his eyebrows.

"Oh, I understand." Not without a fumble. Cue my mind conjuring up all sorts of visions of Rennie and me together in bed.

"Great." He fiddled with the collar of his shirt. "I went to the Egyptian division of the Royal Occult Bureau to consult their library and ask the help of an agent." He growled. "It turned out my choice wasn't wise. Bloody Oliver. He's one of those agents who can cleanse or restore memories, as you have unfortunately learnt."

"Forget Oliver. Tell me about the Unnatural."

His long eyelashes fluttered down his cheeks. "I

believe it's a lamia." If he was expecting a big reaction from me at the mention of the name, he'd be disappointed.

"I've never heard of it."

"I'm not surprised. It's very rare. It's a creature indigenous to Libya. No one knows what it looks like. It takes the shape of the person who'll ignite the fiercest emotion or desire in a human."

"I don't understand." Our knees touched again, and I didn't move my leg but stared boldly at him.

"Do you remember the man who attacked us? You described him as tall with short hair. I saw a lean man with a bald head and sharp teeth. The lamia appears to look different to different people because we don't find the same things frightening, exciting, or attractive."

"Oh." I slouched back. "So when I see Sandro..."

He gave me a sad smile and gazed at the floor. "I believe he embodies the perfect qualities you like in a man, from his looks to his voice and manners. Your ultimate love interest."

Why did the explanation shoot guilt into my heart? "Not necessarily."

He gazed up, his throat working. "You saw a handsome, kind man, though."

Yes, but it was before I met Rennie. "But another person, looking at him, will see a different man."

"Yes. The lamia has a certain degree of control over its features, though. When it wants to charm someone, it will become a charming person for everyone who looks at it, a sort of ideal personality that would satisfy the average person. Sometimes, it can deliberately transform into someone and keep the appearance for a few minutes. It's complicated."

"You didn't seem very charmed by Edward when he introduced himself to us."

He pointed a finger at his eyes. "Men with green eyes are more resilient to the Unnaturals' power. That's why there are so many green-eyed agents at the bureau. Edward didn't charm me, but I didn't suspect he was an Unnatural either."

"But how does a lamia kill?"

"A kiss." His gaze dipped to my lips for a moment that was long enough to set my body on fire.

"But"—this was embarrassing—"I've kissed Sandro many times, and nothing has ever happened."

He glanced at my lips again. "It's not clear how it works, but a lamia is capable of destroying a human with a kiss. What remains of the human is a glob of silver gelatine."

"Mrs Francis!" I'd been so bold with my parents, but the thought of ending up like Mrs Francis, like a blob of goo on the floor, sent a chill down my back.

"Yes. When you found the silver substance, I knew we were dealing with an Unnatural. I didn't know about the lamia. But I don't believe it wants to kill you. It had several opportunities to kill you, but it didn't do it."

I'd kissed a creature who reduced people to gelatine. "Then what does it want?"

He shrugged. "I don't know. But it's obvious it was the

lamia who seduced the real Edward Morrison. He wants to be ravished by you, and the lamia took your shape."

"Goodness me. I don't know how that makes me feel." I shook my head. "So the Scot who attacked Mrs Francis…"

"It was the lamia, taking the shape of her wildest fantasy."

"The Scot on the cover of her book."

He nodded. "It all fits."

We remained in silence while the gondola slowed its pace.

"Do you think it's still on board the SS *Florentia*?" I asked.

"I think it's following you for some reason. It tried to charm you in England. When you left, it followed you, which is unusual for an Unnatural."

"Oh, dear." I scratched my scar absentmindedly.

"Is the scar from the giant eel? Your father told me about your incident." He touched the scar with the tip of his finger, tracing it along my inner wrist.

The simple contact made my spine wilt. "Yes," I whispered.

The strokes became gentler and more curious. His fingers slid under the hem of my sleeve and caressed my skin in small circles.

"You could've died," he said, his voice cracking with emotion. "It was my fault. I shouldn't have left you alone with Oliver. Like an idiot, I believed him when he said he wouldn't hurt you."

"You couldn't know." I sounded husky and breathless.

"It won't happen again." He folded my hand into his and laced his fingers through mine. "The contract I signed—"

"Forget the darn contract. Sod the contract. To hell with it."

His lips parted. "Your parents have been very clear about what they expect from me."

I glowered. "I can make my own choices. I don't need them or you to choose for me."

"They care about you. I care about you. We want to protect you."

"Poppycock. They want to control my future. I won't allow anyone to do that. Not even you."

He kissed my hand. "I'd never do that."

I leant closer. I couldn't help it. He drew in a breath when our lips met midway. A groan rumbled out of him as I ran the tip of my tongue over his lips, taking care not to hurt him. I wanted to unbutton his shirt and run my hands over his smooth skin to feel his hard muscles. I wanted to sit on his lap and tangle my fingers through his hair. The maddening desire pounding through me was a completely foreign sensation to me because what I'd felt for Sandro had an artificial quality that left me a tad cold. But with Rennie, the sensation was stronger and warmer, and I embraced it with my whole heart.

The gondola came to a stop, jolting us. I was an inch away from him, my breath mingling with his.

"I like kissing you," I whisper, staring at his flushed lips.

"So do I." He kissed my hand again, muttering something under his breath before helping me out.

The SS *Florentia* was floating a few miles off the coast to preserve the fragile Venetian coast, thus the passengers had to board a small boat and sail towards the humongous cruise ship. My parents came out of another gondola, their faces darkening with worry as they walked over to me on the dock.

"Are you sure you want to carry on with your plan?" Mother asked me, taking my hands. "You don't have to."

"Yes, I do. The Unnatural is following me. I want to end this affair." I squeezed her hand to strengthen my point, wishing for her to understand.

"Good luck, darling." Father kissed my cheek. "I'm so proud of you," he whispered, bringing tears to my eyes.

"Thank you, Papa."

My parents hugged me fiercely, then gave an equally fierce glare to Rennie.

"Take care of my daughter," Mother said. The 'or else' was implied.

Rennie bowed from the waist. "I'd die for her, madam."

I shot my gaze skywards. How dramatic. But Mother nodded in approval, her face lighting with respect for Rennie.

I waved at my parents as I headed towards the gangplank. When they were out of sight, I suppressed the urge to run after them and tell them to take me home. Running once meant running forever. I needed to face the lamia. It'd made fun of my feelings, playing with me. If I didn't fight back, I'd become its victim, and I'd rather spend my life feeling sick on a ship than become a victim again, scared and isolated. Not anymore.

"What about Edward, Norton, and my charges?" I asked as Rennie and I strode along the main deck.

"The only good thing Oliver did was wipe Edward's, his wife's, and the detective's memories. They don't recall having ever involved you in the incident."

"Good. I have another question. How do we catch the lamia?"

Rennie smiled. "We lure it out."

WHEN RENNIE STAYED in my cabin for the night, I was more than thrilled to have him. It was also part of the plan. A not so complicated plan. The lamia would find me again. We were simply waiting for the right moment to catch it.

After I changed into my nightgown, Rennie locked the door and sat in his usual spot on the floor. But I wasn't going to have any of it.

"Rennie?" I said, sitting up on the bed.

He gazed up.

I patted the place on the bed next to me. "Sleep here. I can't sleep knowing you're on the cold floor."

"Monia—"

"Come here." My voice was low and husky, but commanding. Having regained my memories gave me confidence. "Please. You need to rest properly, and no one has to know. Ever."

He hesitated, chewing his bottom lip. When he rose and uncoiled his powerful body, a tingle started between my thighs. Which didn't make any sense. Or maybe it did. I didn't find him intimidating any longer. I wanted to feel his powerful body against mine. Feel his warmth.

"Are you sure?" he asked, standing next to me, shoulders hunched, as if he wanted to make himself smaller; it wasn't working.

My reply was to pat the empty side of the bed again. The mattress dipped when he sat on the edge to remove his shoes. He stretched next to me over the quilt, all stiff and rigid.

"What's your name?" I asked.

He burst out laughing. "I thought we'd already been introduced."

"I mean your full name." I thumped him on the shoulder. "I'm pretty sure Rennie is short for something."

"Can't you guess what?" He smiled, his body relaxing a little.

"Ronald?"

He scrunched up his face. "Hell, no."

"Robert?"

"Please."

"Rodney?"

He curled up his lip. "It's Lawrence."

"Lawrence," I repeated to taste the name on my tongue. "I love it. Classical and noble."

"Noble my arse. You need to sleep now. You've been weak for a while." He brushed my cheek with his knuckles. "And you need your energy for—"

I wasn't sure where my boldness came from, but I grabbed his hand and kissed it before running the tip of my tongue over his thumb. The shock on his face was so striking it made me chuckle. Desire darkened his gaze as he watched me slide his finger into my mouth. I wrapped my lips around it and sucked on it gently, tasting the saltiness of his skin against the softness of my tongue. A strangled moan rumbled out of him. It was a sound dripping with a dark promise. I slipped his finger between my lips, inch by inch.

I smiled. "Well, I—"

He kissed me hard, pressing his soft, warm mouth against mine. It was a bruising kiss, made of bites and teeth, but it shot heat down to my lower belly and somewhere utterly inappropriate.

His tongue slipped past my lips and explored my mouth with slow strokes. A jolt of desire went through me, causing all of my sensitive spots to pulse with need. I was so focused on him that even the noise of the ship became an indistinct lull. It wasn't like kissing Sandro. The kiss wasn't as perfect as Sandro's kisses. But exactly for that reason, it was raw and wild and filled with crude passion, a battle where we both fought for pleasure, igniting a fierce longing within me. It was real.

Grazing my bottom lip, he broke the kiss and inched away from me. "We shouldn't."

"Who cares?"

Another laugh rumbled out of him. "Who are you, and what have you done with Monia?"

"I've had enough of being a scared woman. That's all. Scared ladies don't get to kiss handsome men like you."

His eyelids drooped. "And of course, learning your perfect lover is actually an Unnatural helped you reach this conclusion." He didn't say those words in a reproachful tone but with sadness. "I understand."

Dash it. Could he be right? No, I'd started to find Sandro's kisses less enticing a while ago. "It's not like that. It took me a bit, but I realised Sandro's kisses didn't spark any flames inside me. My stomach didn't lurch when I was close to him. My skin didn't tingle. Yet when I'm with you, every emotion is amplified, every sensation is intense, so intense I want to sing."

"Please don't."

We both laughed. He kissed my fingers.

I caressed his cheek. "I want you, Rennie. Only you. All of you."

"Monia."

"The kiss you've just given me is the best kiss I have ever received." I licked my bottom lip, savouring the predatory way he looked at me.

"Was it?" He traced the curve of my cheek with a finger. "Even better than Sandro's kisses?"

"There's no comparison. Sandro's kisses were too polite to be passionate."

His fingers trailed down my neck, then over my

shoulder and slid down the sleeve of my nightgown. I drew in a breath as he caressed my collarbone.

"Your skin is so silky," he said, stroking the top of my breasts. His hand went lower and brushed my nipple through the fabric of the nightgown. We both groaned at the contact.

I arched my back, pushing my breast into his hand. He didn't disappoint. He slid his hand under the collar of my nightgown and stroked my breast, skin against skin. His warm breath caressed me as he lowered the nightgown.

In the moonlight, my skin turned a lovely shade of silver, and I watched, fascinated, as he fondled my breasts and tweaked my nipples. Each time he rolled them with his fingers, a jolt of pleasure coursed through me. But when he closed his hot mouth around one, I moaned loudly. His tongue rolled over the taut peak of my breast with devotion and maddening slowness. Instant wetness pooled between my legs. I rocked my hips as he tongued the other nipple while pinching the first. The sensations taking over my body had nothing to do with what I'd experienced with Sandro. Not even close. I was burning, and I wanted more. He changed the rhythm, sucking hard and making me feel his teeth against my sensitive skin. It only fuelled the fire. Flames licked at me between the legs. I couldn't take it anymore.

"Rennie," I begged.

Still sucking at my nipple, he bunched my nightgown up to my hips and slipped a hand between my thighs, finding me wet and hopeless. He rubbed me with gentle fingers, entering them inside my slit and circling my nub with a thumb. I moved my hips against his hand, desperate to get more of the delicious friction. A storm was building up inside me.

And then the release hit me. It thundered through me and turned me into a sensual creature. He didn't stop touching me until I lay satisfied on the bed, breathing hard.

He wrapped his arms around me and pulled me closer. "I'd love to do more, but if the lamia attacks us tonight, I must be ready to fight." He kissed my cheek while his arm coiled around my waist.

"It was amazing." My eyelids grew heavy as the release faded. "I almost wish it came now, so we have the rest of the night to ourselves." I snuggled closer to his chest and closed my eyes, sighing happily. The fatigue of the day dropped on my shoulders, causing me to sag against him.

He caressed the top of my head. "Sleep, Monia. I'll watch over you."

BRIGHT SUNLIGHT FLOODED the dining hall the next morning, but the turquoise sky and the golden light couldn't lift my anxiety.

Last night had been uneventful. No attack had come, which could mean many things. The plan might be too weak, the lamia might have left the ship, or it didn't find me interesting anymore. But if I thought about Rennie's mouth over my nipples and his hand between my legs, everything seemed brighter. My skin tingled deliciously in all the right places, and little shivers ran along my back.

Rennie and I were having breakfast, smiling over our cups of tea whenever our gazes met. A light flush coloured his cheeks, and I wondered if I looked the same, glowing and pink.

"Did you enjoy last night?" He brushed my fingers. The sunlight sparked in his emerald eyes, igniting them with golden specks.

"Do it again," I whispered, pushing aside the thought that we were here for a reason that had nothing to do with my sexual awakening.

"I will." He smiled, lacing my fingers with his.

My mood went from glorious to furious in an instant when Oliver strolled towards us. Even Rennie turned around.

"What is he doing here?" I asked.

Rennie stood up so quickly his chair was almost knocked over.

Oliver didn't flinch but offered me a bow. "Miss Fitzwilliam, it's good to see you well."

"Not thanks to you." I didn't return the greeting.

"Don't you dare talk to her," Rennie hissed, taking a menacing step towards him. "The bureau—"

Oliver held up a hand. "Don't waste your breath. The bureau isn't going to punish me. While you were locked up in a fancy cell, I had a hearing with my superiors. They understood I'd acted for the best. Miss Fitzwilliam is safe, and we're about to catch..." He glanced around and lowered his voice. "A lamia." His eyes glinted as he produced a document from his pocket. "In fact, I have the order to catch the lamia alive."

"Alive?" Rennie and I said together.

"It's such a rare species that the bureau wants to study it. That said"—he grabbed a chair and sat down at the table before taking an oat biscuit from the plate—"how are we going to capture it?"

My mouth dropped open. "I can't believe they didn't punish you. You nearly killed me."

"But you didn't die." He winked at me. The scoundrel. "And let's face it, you wanted your memories back."

Curse him, but he was right. Still, he shouldn't be here, but behind bars.

"The lamia killed a woman," Rennie gritted out. "Dangerous Unnaturals must be stopped, not caught."

As if he hadn't spoken, Oliver drummed his fingers on the table. "It must sleep somewhere on the ship. Not much is known about lamiae, but every creature needs sleep. Where would it sleep?"

He was being absurd. How could we catch a creature no one knew anything about? "Even if we find where it nests, how can we capture it?" I asked, my anger still simmering.

Rennie shot me a reproachful glance, as if to say 'how can you encourage him?'

"Did you know there's a small island called Murano close to Venice?" Oliver popped another biscuit into his mouth.

I wanted to slap him. "Of course. Murano is famous for its tradition of glass-making. And?"

He nodded. "A cage made of iridescent Murano glass will hold the lamia safely inside."

It sounded like a pile of horse dung, in my opinion.

I narrowed my eyes at him. "How do you know that? You said the lamiae are the most mysterious and unknown creatures."

"Well..." He took his time to select another biscuit. I hoped he choked on it. "A glass cage works for two other species similar to the lamia, same genus. It's worth a try."

"A try?" Rennie roared. "I won't risk Monia's life again. If I find the lamia, I'll kill it."

"We have only to search the ship," Oliver concluded, wiping his mouth. "And we'll do our duty, which is what the bureau ordered us to do." He patted a hand over the pocket of his jacket where the document lay. "Delicious biscuits, by the way. They give you the right energy to start a new day."

Rennie and I groaned. As if we hadn't searched the darn ship several times.

THIRTEEN

AND WE DID IT AGAIN. Searching the darn, ruddy ship, only to find absolutely nothing. It wasn't even frustrating at that point, just boring.

As the SS *Florentia* approached Sicily, we spent our days going up and down ladders and stairs and sneaking into narrow passageways slick with engine oil and smelling like sweaty socks. We'd found the cash-filled wallets of two passengers, a wedding ring a lady had lost a while ago, and a seagull eating from the garbage bin in the kitchen. But no trace of the lamia.

Since I refused to spend another hour buried in some obscure passage of the ship on a brilliant June day and since I was still fatigued by my ordeal, I lounged on one of the sunbathing chairs on the main deck, enjoying the warmth and the light on my skin. Curse the lamia. If it wanted me, it knew where to find me.

Oliver paced in front of me, nervous like a father about

to have his firstborn. Rennie sat next to me, elbows on his knees as he followed Oliver's moves with a hawk-like gaze.

"It can't be possible." Oliver ran a hand through his blond hair, snarling. "Where is it? Why didn't it show itself?"

"Maybe it lost interest in me." I closed my eyes and wondered if I would acquire a nice tan. Fashion was so odd. Until a few years ago, tanned skin was considered unfashionable, even vulgar. Pale skin had always been a favourite feature for the ladies. They'd protected their skin from the sun with parasols and cosmetics. But since holidays and cruises to distant places had become popular, so had a tan. A tan meant holidays, holidays meant money, and money meant fun for society, and I actually liked that—

"Did you hear me?" Oliver was scowling at me.

"No." I didn't think I had any obligation to be polite to him.

"I think you should have a look at the conservatory," he said. "We haven't checked it recently, and it's my best bet to find the lamia's nest. Maybe it likes the plants and the warmth."

I rolled my eyes, but before I could answer, Rennie stood up. "Monia is tired because, just in case you forgot, someone had the brilliant idea to traumatise her by forcing her memories out while knowing the procedure could be lethal."

Oliver stepped closer to him. Only a few feet of

charged masculine aggression separated them. "We have already discussed that."

"And you still sound like a bastard for what you did to her." A muscle in Rennie's neck ticked.

As much as I loved that he was standing up for me, I was perfectly able to defend myself. So I rose—groaning inwardly at my ruined sunbath—and stepped between the two stags about to butt heads.

"Gentlemen, please. I can decide for myself." It was becoming my motto and I loved it. I turned towards Rennie. "Rennie, I would like to take a walk. Would you please escort me?"

"I'd be delighted," he said through gritted teeth. Without taking his eyes off Oliver, he took my hand and strode off. "Where would you like to go?" he asked after we had left the main deck.

"The conservatory." I laughed. "I just didn't want to give Oliver the satisfaction of knowing I agreed with him."

He laughed too, his gaze softening.

The conservatory was indeed a beautiful place to spend a sunny day. With its tall ferns, rhododendrons, and orchids, it gave the illusion of being in a jungle. The other good thing was the other passengers snubbed it, for some reason. They preferred the shows at the theatre or the concerts while I found the lush plants and the quiet to be soothing. The scent of jasmine filled the air when we entered the garden. The slosh of water came from a fountain with water lilies floating around.

"You really don't like Oliver, do you?" I asked, taking his arm.

"Do you like him?" A little growl crept into his voice.

"I can't forgive him for having nearly killed me, but to be honest, I'm glad to have my memories back. Finally, my life makes sense. Now I know where the fear and sense of oppression came from." I shook my head. "I regret having asked my parents to cleanse my memories. I shouldn't have done it."

Rennie held my hand tightly. "I want to punch the poncy bastard for what he did to you every time he breathes. But I didn't like him even before the incident. It's a feeling."

We strolled through hibiscus plants with red flowers bigger than my hand and orchids that released a sweet fragrance into the air.

"I find it odd that the bureau wants to capture the lamia alive." I touched one of the flowers. Drops of water glistened on the petals. "Lamiae are rare, but the bureau's priority is people's safety, not research. I don't understand what the bureau is thinking."

"That's a bloody good point." He stroked my hand. "We should take a closer look at the documents he so quickly showed us."

"I agree." The heat and humidity formed a soft mist that veiled the emerald leaves. "Do you think the lamia left?" I asked.

"I don't know. No one knew a lamia could kiss without

killing a person. Everything we've learnt so far is new. Perhaps it'll reappear when it's hungry again."

"How will I know I'm meeting the lamia, if it doesn't appear as Sandro or Edward?"

Rennie paused in front of a spot from where we could see the sea. "I asked your parents the same question when we were in Venice. The reason your mother thought the lamia was an incubus is because its eyes darkened when he was about to kiss you. Do you remember it?"

I thought about that night, weeks ago, when Sandro and I'd been alone at the ball. "When he leant closer, I actually closed my eyes. Then my mother screamed, and when I opened my eyes, Sandro was already leaving. But I didn't see his eyes changing colour. But wait. Yes, it's true. In Tunis, I noticed his eyes becoming glossy and black." I glanced at him. "After we kissed."

His thumb brushed my knuckles in slow, gentle circles that seemed to tell me I was precious to him. "How was it?"

"What?" My breath came out a little quicker.

"Kissing Sandro when you really liked him." His voice lowered.

I shifted my weight. "Well, I have to say it was magical. He looked like my ideal man, straight out of my fantasies. So of course, his kiss was simply perfect. Too perfect now that I think about it."

"Too perfect?" He kept stroking my hand with the rough pad of his thumb.

"The kiss lacked passion or wildness. I knew exactly what and how he was going to do it. He was a product of my imagination, in a way, so his actions were following my own wishes. There was no excitement, no surprise."

"And when I kiss you?" He stepped in front of me, slowly pushing me against the wall.

I loved the rough edge in his husky voice. "It's wild. I'm on the edge all the time, and I like it. Why don't you do it again? You promised you would."

His mouth was over mine in a moment. The kiss didn't start slowly, but like a punishment. The tip of his tongue pried my lips open and explored every inch of my mouth with urgent, confident strokes. When the hard muscles of his chest pressed against my body, my knees weakened. Rennie devoured my mouth with an intense hunger that woke my desire. As his big hands took my waist, he kissed my jaw and neck, whispering my name. My core throbbed, remembering his touch.

"Anyone can see us," he muttered against my skin. His thumb brushed the underside of my breast before stroking my nipple through the fabric of my shirt.

I didn't want him to stop. Even my body didn't want him to stop, if the way my back arched, thrusting my breasts deeper into his palm, was any indication. So I trailed my hand over his inner thigh, heading towards the unmistakable bulge in his trousers.

He sucked in a shaky breath and kissed my collarbone. "This is a dangerous game."

An exciting game. I could become addicted to the way he breathed hard when I touched him. Brushing my lips over a tempting spot on his neck, I stroked his long shaft. It twitched in my hand at the same time as Rennie made a growling noise deep in his throat. I loved that sound. It made me feel desired.

I ran my hand up and down his length, savouring every groan as it left his lips. "I'm curious to know how..." I paused, wondering if I really, really wanted to end the sentence.

He pinched my nipple hard enough to make me moan. "What are you curious about?"

My chest lifted and lowered quickly. "How it would feel inside me."

His growl from before became the most sensual sound I'd ever heard. With deft fingers, he undid the first buttons of my shirt. I pressed my hand over his hard shaft in response, and he paused, closing his eyes and muttering a curse that would have earned him a slap from my mother.

My nipples peaked when he lowered the hems of my shirt and chemise, exposing them to his hungry gaze. Then his mouth covered my breast and his tongue flicked over my aching nipple. The sensation speared through me and heated my core with wet desire. He sucked hard, and each pull caused the throb between my thighs to intensify. It bordered on pain.

In a frenzy, I slid my hand inside his trousers. I was worried he might stop me. But the moment I touched the silky skin of his rock-hard shaft, he hissed and sucked on my nipple harder. He felt even bigger with my hand touching his naked skin. Steel sheathed in silk. I had to squeeze my thighs together to ease the ache between them at the thought of him sliding inside me, stretching me.

I was going to die in a pool of pleasure. "Please," I said, although I had no idea what I was pleading for. "Please."

He bunched my skirts and lifted them to my waist while tonguing my nipples. Then his rough fingers were stroking the delicate skin of my inner thighs, and I stopped breathing for a moment. His hips rubbed against my hand. If possible, his shaft grew bigger as I gently ran my hand up and down it while rubbing the blunt head with my thumb. I didn't know what I was doing, but it didn't seem to matter.

I gasped when his fingers found the spot that ached the most. He caressed it gently with slow circles, spilling a burning sensation into my body. I rocked my hips until we were both moving while touching each other, stealing kisses and biting our lips.

His hard finger entered me and stroked a spot deep inside me. A crescendo of sensations was flaming through my body. The conservatory disappeared as I focused only on Rennie's scent and touch. I was on the verge of a monumental cliff. At a flick of his tongue over my nipple, energy burst inside me. I was shattered by the strength of my feelings and sagged against him. But he wasn't finished with me.

He slid his fingers in and out of me, rubbing and

kissing me harder. His hands, lips, and tongue were suddenly everywhere on my body, making me squirm again and making me moan his name until he wrung out of me another powerful release. White flashes danced in front of me with the pleasure. Only then, his assault slowed. He watched me, a light of triumph in his eyes.

"Who makes you feel better now?" he asked, still stroking my wet, sensitive core.

"It's not a competition," I said among pants.

"Maybe." He pinched my little nub and tweaked it, making me shudder with need again. "But I want an answer."

"I don't know." I was wheezing. "I'm not sure."

"You aren't sure?" He pressed the pad of his thumb over my nub while rolling my nipple between his lips. His teeth grazed the swollen tip of my breast while his fingers were sliding in and out of me. The third release shuddered through me so hard my knees nearly buckled. He held me upright, scattering kisses over my breasts.

"Well? Do you have an answer now?" he asked.

"You," I said, breathless. "Only you."

He kissed me again, sucking my bottom lip into his mouth and grazing it with his teeth. Then his fingers were between my thighs again, doing their magic while playing with my nub and stroking the spot inside me that made me shudder. I didn't think it was possible, but energy built up inside me again! The new release—I wasn't sure what number it was—rocked me so hard I bit Rennie's lips and squeezed his fingers between my thighs. The pleasure was too much. My legs were trembling. Only his arm around my waist kept me on my feet.

Exhausted, I reclined my head, closing my eyes. Could someone die from too much pleasure? Rennie scattered sweet kisses on my face. His stubble scratched my skin, sending tiny thrills of pleasure down my spine.

"Oh, Lord." I put my hands on his shoulders.

He chuckled against my skin, buttoning my shirt and adjusting my skirt. "This is only a taste of what I'd like to do to you."

His words caused more wetness to pool between my legs. "My goodness," I muttered, inhaling deeply.

His teeth trapped my earlobe and gave it a little yank. "If I could, I'd eat you between your legs, lapping at your sweet honey until you forget your name, and my name is the only thing you remember. Then I'd thrust inside you to make you feel how much I want you." He took my hand and placed it over the straining evidence of his desire trapped within his trousers. "I want to draw out every last ounce of pleasure from you. And dammit, you're so responsive, I want to take you for a week straight until my cock hurts, until you're so satisfied you'll feel me inside you even after I've finished with you."

My heart was racing. No one had ever talked to me like that. And it was darn exciting.

"Would you let me take you from behind?" he continued mercilessly. "Let me pinch your nipples while I pound inside you from behind? Will you ride me naked? I want you to swallow me whole as well, see your pretty lips around my cock."

I nodded. My mouth hung open, and my brain burst with wild visions. Nodding was all I could do since my tongue had been shocked into silence.

Smirking with all the power of the seven sins, he kissed me softly. "One day, you'll be mine, and I yours."

"One day?" That was a bit too vague. My burning lady bits didn't like vagueness. They wanted to know when he was going to do all those delicious things to me, possibly on a date in the immediate future. "Tell me when."

It was amazing how his features could go from 'lost in lust' to professional in a fraction of a second. I was sure I looked dishevelled, with my cheeks flushed, lips kiss-swollen, and hair rumpled. Not professional at all.

"You know I can't say when." He cupped my cheek. "I'm on duty, technically, and I've already taken too many liberties with you."

"But what we've done here... I quite liked it."

He laughed and kissed me again. "I'm glad you did, and I promise it won't be the last time."

I was pouting. Shamelessly. "I'm not happy with that. It's still too vague."

He kissed my hand. "When this is over, I'll court you with your parents' blessing."

"Sod my parents' blessing." I was surprised by the audacity of my own words. But I meant them. "Mother will never give you her blessing. She's too protective of me and too snobbish for that."

"Monia." Again that warning note in his voice. "I've already crossed a line. I shouldn't touch you. I won't touch you again."

"Is that a challenge?"

His brow shot up. "It's a promise."

So it was a challenge.

FOURTEEN

RENNIE KEPT HIS word for the rest of the day.

Curse him.

That night, when he sat on the floor in my cabin, he didn't touch me, didn't kiss me, and didn't do anything. I was still basking in the post-bliss of our rather pleasurable encounter in the conservatory; thus I didn't try to seduce him. Besides, I wasn't completely sure how to start seducing him. Not to mention, I'd die of embarrassment if he rejected me.

"Are you all right?" he asked, lowering a document he'd been reading. "You keep wringing your hands and shifting."

"Don't you want to sleep next to me?"

His face hardened. "No."

"You're lying."

"And you should be sleeping."

"I'm not—"

The knock on the door shut me up.

"Er, Mr Steele?" Norton asked from the other side of the door. "I'm terribly sorry to trouble you, but there's been an incident."

Rennie was on his feet before I could grab my dressing gown. He opened the door a crack. "What happened?"

"One of the passengers." Norton lowered his voice. "Mrs Morrison, she claimed you, er, didn't behave like a gentleman to her."

"What?" Rennie's roar echoed in the cabin at the same time as I said, "Preposterous."

It was the lamia. I tied the sash of my dressing gown and jumped off the bed.

"I need to ask you a few questions," Norton said. "If you follow me to my office, I'll be very grateful."

"Of course." Rennie put the documents in his bag and threw an exasperated glance at me.

The moment he shut the door behind him, I changed into the first dress I could grab and rushed towards Oliver's cabin. I was wheezing by the time I ran up two levels and down the longest corridor in the world. My body was still recovering.

"Oliver?" I knocked on his door none-too-gently.

"Miss Fitzwilliam?" he asked from the other side. He opened the door, fully dressed in his grey suit. "Is something the matter?" His hair stuck out in every direction, as if he'd run his hands through it several times.

I brushed past him to enter his cabin. "Can I have a word with you in private?"

"What is it?" he said, closing the door behind him.

"The lamia. It attacked Mrs Morrison disguised as Rennie. Detective Norton is interrogating him."

"Excellent." A slow grin stretched his lips. "Where was Mrs Morrison attacked?"

"I don't know, but I need your memory power to help Rennie."

A scoff left him as he threw a dismissive hand up. "Rennie can wait. I want to see the woman first."

"But if you help Rennie first, we can go together to see Mrs Morrison."

"Where is Mrs Morrison?"

Anger burned the back of my mouth. "I don't know."

"Useless wench." With those kind words, he opened the door and strode away.

"Useless rakehell." Curse him for breathing.

Still annoyed at Oliver, I ran towards Norton's office. The least I could do was offer Rennie an alibi.

I knocked on the door. "Detective Norton? It's Miss Fitzwilliam."

He opened the door and welcomed me into his office with a bow. "Miss Fitzwilliam, please take a seat."

Jaw tense, Rennie rose from his chair when I entered. The emerald in his eyes had a stormy quality that spoke of poorly concealed wrath.

Norton clasped his hands behind his back. "Perhaps you can help me convince Mr Steele to cooperate."

"Why? What's the matter?" I asked, sitting next to him.

"You shouldn't be here." Rennie gave a nod towards the door.

I guessed he meant I should be chasing the lamia? But I wasn't going to leave him alone.

"I apologise for the straightforwardness of my question," Norton said, adjusting his glasses. "But can you confirm Mr Steeles has been with you all evening?"

Oh, bother. Was that all? Had Rennie refused to confirm he'd been in my cabin to protect my honour? "Yes, he has been in my cabin all evening."

"Thank you, madam." Norton shot a glare at Rennie. "I was just saying to your... cousin that—"

"Sir." A member of the staff barged in. "Sir, I'm sorry, but it's the Morrisons again. Mr Morrison said a man tried to enter his cabin."

"Good gracious. What's happening today?" Norton wiped his forehead with a handkerchief. "Please wait here." He shut the door with a thud.

"The lamia?" Rennie asked.

"Oliver went after it. He very rudely refused to help you and preferred going to find Mrs Morrison. I guess he's the man who tried to enter their cabin."

"What a mess." He rubbed his forehead. "I didn't want to involve you."

"That's very kind of you, but what's the point of protecting me if Oliver can fix memories in a heartbeat?"

A muscle in his jaw ticked. "That's true. Still, I don't like it. Especially after what happened today. Between us."

I took his face and forced him to stare at me. "I hope what happened today will happen again."

His Adam's apple bobbed up and down as he swallowed. "So do I."

The door was flung open, and Norton strode inside. A sheen of sweat covered his forehead. "Mr Steele, Miss Fitzwilliam, I'm afraid you'll have to follow me."

What now? I fell into step next to Rennie as we left the office and headed towards the back of the ship. Norton led us below deck, past the second-class cabins, and towards the engine room. I'd inspected the SS *Florentia* so many times I had a pretty clear idea of her layout. And bother! I was even starting to address the ship as 'she' as sailors did. One couldn't be more intimate than that with a ship.

"Where are we going?" Rennie asked as we climbed down another ladder.

While the upper levels were pristine and fresh, the bowels of the ship were dark, smelly, and noisy.

"The cargo hold," Norton replied. "There's something I wish to show you."

The hairs on the back of my neck stood on end. There was a note of sheer excitement in Norton's voice that started a chill in my body. And there was something else. Something I couldn't place. A high-pitched ringing I'd never heard before in Norton's voice.

I took Rennie's hand and paused. "I don't like this," I whispered.

"Neither do I." He pushed me behind him. "Norton, what is the meaning of this?"

In a movement too fast for a human eye to catch, the detective leapt and attacked Rennie, which meant he attacked me as well. I fell over backwards, crushed by the combined weights of Rennie and Norton pressing against me.

Pain burned in my back when I hit the floor. Rennie grunted and shoved Norton. Or rather, Sandro. His facial muscles trembled, as if he were having a seizure. His features changed again to those of Edward. Dash it, it was the lamia.

Precious air rushed into my lungs when the weight lifted from my chest. As I picked myself up on unsteady legs, Rennie and the lamia were engaged in a quick fight in the confined space of the narrow passageway. A crack opened on the wall when Rennie slammed the lamia against it. I had no idea Rennie could generate so much violence... and look so incredibly erotic in the process. His muscles snapped and contracted. His face was scrunched up in concentration. His movements were sharp and precise. He was a sight to behold. It wasn't my fault if wetness pooled between my thighs. Rennie himself had told me I was very responsive. I hadn't been sure what he'd meant by that, but I knew it now. I was easily aroused by him, and I wasn't going to apologise for it.

But the lamia seemed to be a good match, especially since it kept changing form. One moment it was Norton, the next a tall, bald man with sharp teeth, then a huge furry creature. Rennie ducked blows and parried punches until there was a popping noise, like that of a champagne bottle being uncorked, and the lamia vanished, leaving only a glittering silver trail behind.

Panting, Rennie stood in the middle of the corridor, fists up. Blood oozed from a cut on his chin. "Hellfire."

I staggered towards him. "Are you all right?"

He wiped his chin. "Just surprised. I didn't expect the lamia to be so strong or quick." He brushed my cheek, roaming his gaze over me. "How are you? Are you hurt?"

"My back is sore, but aside from that, I'm all right." I leant into his touch.

He sucked in a breath that strained his waistcoat. Sweaty and ruffled by the fight, he was even more handsome than usual. Had he always been so attractive? His features were the same, his nose was still crooked, and his body was still powerful. But I would be lying if I said I didn't wish to feel his hands on me again. Or his mouth. He didn't frighten me anymore.

He cleared his throat and withdrew his hand. "We'd better return to Norton's office before he thinks I want to escape justice."

Or before I begged him for a tumble.

FIFTEEN

I DIDN'T LIKE the look on Norton's face after Oliver had cleansed his memories for the second time in the span of a few days. The good detective's eyes were glassy, and the pale colour of his cheeks wasn't reassuring.

Even Mrs Morrison and her husband were ashen and hollow-cheeked after the memory cleansing was over. It hadn't escaped my notice that, if the lamia had turned into Rennie to charm Mrs Morrison, it meant she'd been fantasising about him. I wasn't being jealous, but she was a married woman, for Pete's sake! It was hardly appropriate behaviour for a wife, especially during her honeymoon.

Also, I didn't like the way Oliver yelled at us as he paced in my cabin. Drops of spittle shot out of his mouth every time he shouted. "How could you have let the lamia escape?" he roared. "You had the perfect opportunity to trap it."

"It's bloody fast!" Rennie roared back. "And if you had come to Norton's office, as Monia had asked you, you would've been there to join the fight."

"How the hell are we going to find it now?" Oliver's eyes were nearly bulging out of their sockets. If he kept it up, his brain was going to explode.

But I had to admit he had a point. We hadn't guessed Norton was the lamia until it was too late, and we had no idea how to catch the beast. We were unprepared. The only good news was that at least the lamia was still on board, obviously.

"We have time," I said. "The lamia is still here and is still following me. It followed me to Tunis. It might follow me even to Catania when we arrive in Sicily."

I wasn't being completely honest. The SS *Florentia* was approaching the port of Catania, and after the awful night and Oliver's yelling, my wish to take a stroll on *terra firma* and leave the ship had little to do with catching the lamia. Also, I had no intention of undertaking another useless inspection of the ship. I was steering Oliver's attention away from our failed attempt.

"What do you suggest then?" Oliver asked.

"I can take a stroll through Catania and see what happens." I shrugged.

Surprisingly, Oliver nodded. "Don't make mistakes this time."

Rennie shot forwards. "You bloody cur—"

"It's all right." I grabbed his thick wrist and tugged at it.

"We've already had a fight. The sun is going to rise in a few hours, and I'd rather sleep for a while before we arrive in Sicily."

Nostrils flaring, Oliver and Rennie faced each other until their bodies slackened.

"See you later then," Oliver said, striding out of my cabin.

I exhaled and sat on the bed, kicking off my shoes. "What a night."

He sat next to me and took my hands. "Are you sure you're all right? Do you need anything?"

I smiled. "Actually, I do."

"Tell me." His lips brushed a sweet kiss over my knuckles.

Before I lost my nerve, I kissed him, pulling him closer by the lapels of his jacket. His chest rose, and his lips parted. I slipped my tongue inside his mouth and caressed his, enjoying the delicious shivers his touch sent down my body. He broke the kiss, cupping my face. "I'm on duty. On duty to protect you, and I haven't done a good job so far."

"I understand," I said with forced sweetness, because I didn't understand at all.

He'd done an excellent job so far. I was alive and well. So I rose from the bed and undid my chignon, letting my long strands of hair fall to my waist. He watched me with big eyes as I unfastened my skirt. I swayed my hips in what I thought was a suggestive manner and not the movement of someone who had sprained an ankle. My skirt and petticoats fell to the floor and pooled in a froth of silk and satin.

"Monia." The warning lacked strength though.

After I unbuttoned my shirt, I lowered the sleeves down my arms until I was standing in only my drawers and chemise in front of him. Judging by the way he was focused on me and his trousers growing tighter, my seduction plan was working. I strolled to him, slowly, trying to control my breathing.

"You promised to do a lot of wild things to me," I whispered, removing my chemise. Cool air hit my breasts, hardening their tips.

He licked his bottom lips. "Monia." There was only passion in his voice this time.

I stopped in front of him, then turned around and bent forwards, smiling at his groan. With trembling fingers, I unfastened the drawers and let them slip down my legs. I stepped out of them. It was the first time I'd stood naked in front of a man. His arms wrapped around me from behind, tearing a gasp out of me.

"You don't know what you've started," he said, brushing his lips against my neck.

I moaned when he cupped my breasts and caressed my nipples while biting the curve of my shoulder. A storm of pleasant tingles ran through my body. His hand travelled lower, over my belly, to stop between my legs. He parted my wet folds and groaned when he stroked my nub, pinching it between his fingers. The hard wall of his chest and his erection pressed against my back. His arms caged me and his hands roamed over my body, touching, caressing, and teasing.

He slid one finger inside me, then another, stretching me. When he added a third finger, I sagged against him. With his thumb rubbing my nub and his other hand rolling my nipple, I didn't last long. A scream ripped out of my lips. My inner muscles clenched with little spasms that amplified the release. I sagged against him, utterly spent.

He kissed my neck. "Are you happy now?"

"You promised to take me from behind."

A low chuckle rumbled from him. "Oh, I will, Monia. I will." He lifted me and laid me on the bed, face down. Taking me by the hips, he pulled me onto all fours.

"What are you—" The rest of the sentence was cut off by my gasps as his hot mouth found my wet entrance.

Pleasure was going to kill me. He didn't show any mercy as his tongue delved deeper, teasing, licking, and stroking. My arms were growing weaker the more he lapped at me until I shivered with a release powerful enough to make me scream. As I dropped to the bed, shivering with pleasure, he kept up his sweet assault, adding two thick fingers and hooking them inside me. It was a battle of tongue, lips, and fingers as he rubbed at me endlessly. I writhed underneath him as a new release started to get closer.

I grabbed a fistful of bed sheets as the combined attention of his tongue and fingers sent me over the cliff. The pillow muffled my scream. Slowly, Rennie withdrew his fingers and gave one last stroke with his expert tongue. He kissed his way up to my neck and pulled the quilt over me.

But I wanted to touch him.

"You should rest." Whatever else he wanted to add was cut off by his gasp as I closed my hand around him. He was about to say something else, but I stroked his length gently, up and down, from the smooth tip to the base.

He closed his eyes and reclined his head, and I loved watching him lose control because I was touching him. He was so thick that I could barely contain him in my hand. The more I worked his shaft, the more he growled. I sped up, and his reaction was immediate. Every muscle in his body became taut. It was mesmerising to watch.

A shudder went through him as the warm ribbons of his release soaked my hand. He bared his teeth, his body shaking with the power of the pleasure I was giving him.

"Did you like it?" I asked.

He let out a raspy laugh. "Perfect." He kissed my temple before taking a towel and the basin with soapy water.

If I didn't know better, I'd say her was embarrassed as he wiped my hand clean.

"I want to do it again," I said, scattering kisses to his face.

He returned the kisses. "'Tis but the beginning. But I need to stay focused now."

"Rennie," I complained.

"Let me do my job." He wrapped his arms around me

and lay on the bed next to me. "I promise I'm going to take you properly."

With his whispered words that promised all sorts of debauchery, I closed my eyes.

———

WAKING UP IN Rennie's arms, my body deliciously sore, I couldn't stop beaming. Instead, Rennie wore his usual frown as he finished buttoning his waistcoat.

"Why are you so forlorn?" I asked, taming my wild hair into a bun.

He exhaled without releasing the tension in his neck. "I just wish this situation was over and done with. Between the lamia and Oliver, the mission is turning out more stressful than necessary."

I stood up and hugged him, resting my cheek over his heart. "We'll find a way to catch the lamia, and Oliver will get what he deserves. May I ask you something?"

"Of course." He kissed the top of my head.

"If the lamia shows our desires and our most desperate fears, then who is the tall, bald man who attacked us? What does he mean to you?"

He opened his mouth, but a knock on the door cut him off.

"Miss Fitzwilliam, Rennie?" Oliver's voice came through the door. "We're about to dock. Are you ready to leave?"

Rennie's gaze shot skywards. "Curse him."

I waved a dismissive hand. "Ignore him. Tell me what bothers you."

He took my hands and pressed them against his chest, letting me feel the steady beat of his heart. "Let's catch the lamia."

Twenty minutes later, we were waiting in line to leave the SS *Florentia* and land on Sicilian soil. I'd seen the Andes when I'd travelled with my parents in South America. Tall, majestic volcanoes topped with snow. Nevertheless, the sight of Mt Etna, towering over the city and blowing out white puffs of smoke, captured my full attention. The scent of orange blossoms and seawater filled the air. Warm sunlight stroked my cheeks, and a breeze cool enough to be pleasant shuffled my hair.

Rennie smiled and tucked a strand of my hair behind my ear. "You look happy."

"Thanks to you."

He inched closer and paused before kissing me. Clearing his throat, he drew back. "Let's not cause a scandal."

"Oh, I'd love a scandal. Afterwards, we'll have to—" I coughed into my closed fist. Dash it, what was I thinking? Trapping Rennie into a marriage wasn't something I wanted.

"We'll have to?" he asked, squeezing my hand.

"Nothing." I straightened. "I don't want you to have the wrong impression."

His warm breath feathered over my cheek. "I would marry you, anyway. Scandal or not."

A warm, fluttery feeling filled my chest. He beamed, the sunlight gilding his skin. It wasn't a proposal, but at least I knew his intentions. I kept smiling while we walked along the gangplank and reached the city. Oliver would follow Rennie and me at a distance not to alarm the lamia. A useless precaution, but I was glad he wasn't close enough to hear us.

Buildings made from black lava stones gleamed like obsidian jewels in the bright sunlight, reminding me of the Royal Occult Bureau but with sunshine. There were palm trees and hedgerows, fountains, and flowerbeds like in any other garden I'd visited, but with a touch of wildness. The flowers showed intense colours. The scents were too strong. The trees were too tall.

Oliver brushed past us, hissing. "Don't play tourist. Focus on the mission."

Before I could ask him what he meant by that, he marched away.

"Oliver is obsessed with that lamia," I said, as we promenaded along a path in Bellini Garden, through pine trees and manicured flowerbeds.

"The lamia killed a woman and is threatening to kill again," Rennie said. "Any agent worth his salt would want to catch it. But I agree, he's too obsessed with it."

I scratched the back of my neck, a nagging sensation tugging at it. "I don't like the fact the lamia could be anywhere without us realising it. It could be watching us right this minute."

"That's the point of our stroll."

A wide gravel path snaked its way through tall trees and trimmed bushes. We took a lateral trail leading to a folly. Ivy covered several alcoves, the green leaves and stems coiling around the marble pillars. A sign written in English, French, and Italian informed us that we were in the lovers' nooks. My word, it would be impossible for a couple of lovers to be spotted inside one of those nooks. Two people would be perfectly protected and hidden from prying eyes. Wonderful.

I nudged Rennie with an elbow. "Would you like to try?" I was becoming insatiable.

"We should be careful." His warning lacked anger, but he wasn't gazing at me. He was searching the bushes.

"Spoilsport. Only five minutes."

He frowned. "No."

Annoying man. "You can be very boring when—"

He took my elbow and dragged me towards a nook.

"Yes!" I giggled when we were both tucked inside a nice alcove.

"Shush." He pressed a finger against my lips and tilted his head towards the path.

I peeked through the dense vegetation, but aside from statues and more bushes, there wasn't much to see. "What is it? I don't see anything."

"Wait." His arm coiled around my waist and pulled me closer to his hard body.

Oliver emerged from a corner. The lapels of his jacket were pulled up over his face. Another man came out from behind the hedgerow. Rennie's fingers tensed around me. The two men threw glances around, loitering.

"I told you not to contact me here," Oliver hissed.

"Have you found it?" the man asked.

"Not yet. There has been a complication." Oliver shoved his hands into his pockets, searching the path.

The man spat on the ground and shook his head. "I can't wait forever. The deal is going to end in a few days. I've been patient, but you haven't given me any results. You won't see a penny unless you bring it to me."

A hard glint flashed in Oliver's gaze. "I'll find it. Don't worry."

They lowered their voices, and I didn't understand what they were saying. After a quick nod of their heads, they strode away in opposite directions.

"What was that?" I whispered, even though Rennie and I were alone.

"I have a hunch."

"Do you think the man was talking about the lamia?" I turned around to stare at him.

"We can't be sure, but it makes sense. I guess Oliver doesn't want to catch the lamia because the bureau ordered him to, but to sell it."

"What a crook."

He wrapped his other arms around me. "He should be expelled from the bureau."

"Do they expel agents who kiss on duty?" I ran my hand over his chest, wondering how it'd feel without his clothes.

"Careful." His usual warning note rang in his voice, but I ignored it and kept touching him.

"Just one kiss."

"I don't think I can give you only one kiss." His hand slid down my bottom. "If I start kissing you, I won't stop. You know that."

There was only one way to test that. Flexing up onto my tiptoes, I pressed my lips against his. He didn't yield. His lips remained sealed. I ran the tip of my tongue over the seam and pried his mouth open. Still, he wasn't reciprocating, and I felt like I was forcing him. I didn't want to—Oh, my word! Passion erupted out of him with a deep, hard kiss that stole my breath. His expert tongue punished my mouth with long lashes while his hands grabbed the globes of my bottom and squeezed, pulling me to him and making me feel the strength of his erection.

He shoved me against the wall of the nook and kissed me with his teeth, tongue, and punishing lips. It was almost a fight for control. We were both breathing hard when we broke the kiss.

"My Lord," I muttered. "Why do I shake with pleasure when you kiss me?"

Rennie tugged at the hem of his jacket to cover his trousers where a growing problem was evident. He took my face in his hands, his chest brushing mine. "If I didn't know you were human, I'd believe you were a succubus who ensnared my senses."

Perhaps I was a shallow girl, but the fact I had that power over him made me feel beautiful and graceful. He rubbed his thumb over my bottom lip slowly, squashing the soft skin as he went.

"We'd better leave this nook before I do something we'll both regret later," he said.

He held my hand and dragged me out of the nook. As we walked along the path, he laced his fingers through mine in an intimate gesture. A small fluttery feeling blossomed in my chest.

I rested my head on his shoulders. "You look brooding. Not that I don't like it, but what bothers you?"

He stopped under the shadow of a baroque building. "There's something I need to tell you."

The seriousness in his voice caused me to whip my head up. A cold sensation dropped into my stomach. "Oh, dear. You have a betrothed, don't you? A wife? A child?"

"No!" His eyebrows knitted together. "I would've never kissed you if I'd had an intended. What kind of cur do you think I am?"

I let out a breath. "Don't be offended. I just thought you were too good to be true."

His expression softened. He kissed my cheek, his stubble scratching my skin. "It's not about another woman."

"Then what is it?" I kissed his hand.

"It's about the question you asked me earlier, about that man." He stiffened.

"Yes?" I prompted him when he didn't add anything.

He searched around. "The lamia looked like one of my tutors at Sheltenham Academy. Not identical, or I would've realised he was an Unnatural, but it had the same slimy features as him."

Future occult agents were admitted to Sheltenham Academy at the age of eleven. A brutal training practice would turn them into junior agents by the age of seventeen. Father had told me horrifying stories of having been beaten by his teachers, left in the cold for entire nights, or flogged. Speaking of which, now I understood why my parents had put 'flogging' into the contract with Rennie. Father had been raised in Sheltenham. Punishments and threats were something he understood. Female agents were trained in a girls' college no less brutal.

"What did he do to you?" I asked, as we strolled along the pavement in Via Etnea.

He shrugged. "Nothing the other students didn't also endure. The usual. Beating, hitting, and whipping."

Usual? I didn't like the way he so casually talked about abuse. "But?"

"He was particularly brutal to me." He clenched his jaw. "I reacted once when he was beating me, and he never forgot it. One night he..." He glanced at me. "I've changed my mind. You don't need to know it."

"I want to." I wanted to share whatever burden he was carrying. "We decided to know each other better, remember?"

"Maybe certain things are better left unknown." He stroked my cheek.

"What did that monster do to you?"

He remained silent for a few minutes. I worried he

didn't want to speak further. His Adam's apple bounced up and down. "He dragged me out of bed and beat me with a wooden stick until the only thing I could do was kneel in front of him."

"Oh, Rennie."

"That's not all." His hand shook, and his lips paled. "He said I was weak and pathetic, and if I wanted to be a real agent, I had to toughen up, do as he said, and accept my punishment. And so I did. Only it made me feel even more alone and afraid of him."

Horror burned like acid in my veins. A flare of anger flushed to my head. "Did you tell—"

"Of course not!" he said.

"Sorry, I didn't mean to upset you."

He pinched the bridge of his nose. "I should apologise. I didn't mean to be brusque to you. It's just I've never talked about it with anyone, and although the education in Sheltenham is brutal, it's never been like that. I should've reported him, but I was twelve and didn't want to disappoint my parents by whining about my tutor. So I steered away from him and learnt not to attract attention to myself. I didn't realise what had happened was wrong until later on when I understood what he'd done to me. I can't say the knowledge made things better, but..." He swallowed again, a tendon in his neck throbbing.

I cupped his cheek. "I understand. You don't have to add anything else."

He nodded. His lips pressed in a grim line, and eyelashes fluttered over his cheeks.

"What happened to him?"

"He was killed by an Unnatural years later. I didn't shed any tears."

I wrapped my arms around his neck and hugged him. He held me back, burying his face in the crook of my neck. Something cracked in my chest. Guilt for having ever considered him harsh and cold gnawed at me. Tenderness towards the boy, who had been abused, and a desire to comfort him caused my pulse to stutter. The urge to protect him from further pain surged.

He didn't say anything, but held me, gripping me close to him. His embrace was nearly painful, but I wouldn't ask him to release me for anything in the world. We held each other until our breaths mingled, and our heartbeats became one. The hug was more intimate than the fumbles we'd shared, more touching than our passionate kisses, and more binding than a promise of marriage. There was no doubt in my mind or in my soul. I was his. I belonged to this man and his brave heart. I wanted him in my life.

I wasn't sure how much time had passed when we released each other, slowly and without being able to untangle our fingers, but it seemed the embrace had lasted both too long and not enough. Our souls exchanged a conversation in the hug, more precious than any token of love.

We boarded the SS *Florentia* in silence, walking hand in hand. His shoulders were hunched, and his head hung over his chest.

I kissed his cheek. "Don't be embarrassed."

"What do you think of me now?"

Oh, Lord. He looked like a lost boy, seeking approval.

"That you're a wonderful, brave man," I said, kissing him softly on the lips. "And I hope to spend more time in a lovers' nook with you."

A slow smirk, not boyish at all but all manly, quirked up a corner of his mouth. "It's a deal."

I nodded. "A deal."

He gave me a quick kiss. "Now, let's search Oliver's cabin before he returns on board."

SIXTEEN

AS WE WALKED along the corridor towards Oliver's cabin, Norton brushed past us, his glasses askew on his nose.

He offered a bow, a daft smile on his face. "Good afternoon, Miss Williams, Mr Satchwell."

"Actually, we are... never mind. Thank you, Detective." I bobbed a curtsy.

"Goodbye." He trotted away, waving a hand.

I winced, watching him as he muttered under his breath. "Will he return to normal?"

"Give him a few weeks, and he'll be better." Rennie knocked on Oliver's door. "Oliver?" When no reply came, he picked the lock with a metallic rod faster than I could say 'thief.'

"That's impressive."

He grinned. "An agent's basic skill."

Since Oliver was double-crossing us, I felt no shame or guilt about rifling through his room.

The air was thick with the smell of Oliver's cologne. It wasn't unpleasant, but it was one of those perfumes that stuck in one's nostrils for a long time. Like Rennie, Oliver had a meticulously organised room. Shirts and trousers were neatly folded in a pile. His shoes formed a row in the wardrobe, and his shaving kit sparkled, as if recently scrubbed.

"Do they teach you how to be perfectly tidy in Sheltenham?" I asked, opening the drawer of the nightstand. "My father is the same. All order and tidiness."

"The cadets are punished if they leave their clothes around the dormitory. Messy rooms aren't tolerated. Unshaven chins are considered an abomination. And table manners have to be excellent."

"Hades, is there anything the cadets aren't punished for?"

He paused while searching the dresser, brows drawing together. "I don't think so. Maybe only for not... No, I can't think of anything."

"I was joking. Oh, leave it." A folder fell to the floor when I rummaged through a satchel.

A document with the Royal Occult Bureau's symbol spilt out of it. The paper was the formal authorisation to catch the lamia alive. All the stamps and signatures from the British office of the bureau in Cairo filled the document.

"Rennie, come here."

His heat enveloped me when he stood next to me.

I pointed at the bureau's symbol, the crown with the letters 'R. O. B.' underneath. "I think this is a forged document. The gold of the crown isn't as shiny as it should be. I remember that, when I was a child, I was mesmerised by the way the crown shone in the light, reflecting the colours of a rainbow when tilted at the right angle. Father told me it was printed with a special type of ink to recognise counterfeit documents."

He took the paper and inspected it in the sunlight. "I think you're right. It's a good imitation, but not perfect. It doesn't mean Oliver is doing anything illegal, though."

"How can you say that?" I expected a little more enthusiasm from him. "He forged a paper."

"Maybe someone tricked him, and he honestly thought the document was genuine."

I pouted. "I don't believe it."

"Neither do I, but a man is innocent until proven guilty. We need stronger evidence than this."

My shoulders slumped. "We'll keep searching, then."

He took my chin and tilted it up. "You've done a brilliant job." He brushed his lips against mine, too chastely for my liking.

Before he could pull away, I dug my fingers into his thick hair and held him close for a proper kiss. He responded immediately. His arms circled my waist, and his tongue darted over my lips. The stubble on his chin scratched my cheek when he tilted his head to deepen the kiss. It wasn't my fault if wetness dampened my drawers.

Rennie had the power to ignite my lust with a single, fierce kiss.

The metallic scraping noise coming from the door jolted us. Someone was entering. Rennie took my hand and shoved me under the bed. We snuggled closer as the door opened and someone entered. Judging by the new cloud of perfume hitting my senses, it was Oliver.

"Hell," he muttered.

When he plonked down onto the bed, the mattress dipped, nearly touching my head. I shot a horrified glance at Rennie and pointed at the forged documents I had left on the nightstand. Rennie gave the slightest shrug.

Oliver removed his shoes and set them in a line next to the nightstand. The bed groaned as he shifted. Then there was silence. He shot to his feet, and the springs in the mattress uncoiled with a snap. A growl came from him.

"Son of a bitch."

Dash it. He must have seen the documents. I clamped a hand over my mouth.

He paced with long strides, muttering. My nose was tickling from the dust on the floor. I took a deep breath and held it, forcing my muscles to remain still. Instead, Rennie didn't seem to have any trouble staying motionless. His gaze was focused on Oliver's feet and his body was tense, but he didn't look like he'd swallowed wasps, like I was sure I did.

Minutes passed. Oliver stopped pacing. When he slid his shoes on, I wanted to cheer. The moment he left the room, Rennie helped me out of our hiding place and coiled an arm around me as we hurried towards the door. We didn't speak until we were out of the cabin.

"I'm sorry." He gave my hand a gentle squeeze. "I shouldn't have been distracted."

"I distracted you. So it's my fault. Where do you think Oliver went?"

"I'll follow him." We stopped in front of my cabin. "Stay here. I'll be back as soon as possible."

"See you later."

He kissed my cheek before dashing away.

I washed, changed, and read a book, but after an hour, I grew worried about Rennie. What was he doing? Should I search for him? Maybe Oliver caught up with him. I fiddled with my hands, wondering if I should ask Norton, when there was a knock at the door.

"Monia?"

My traitorous heart gave a kick at the sound of Rennie's voice.

"You're back." I opened the door and beamed. "Did you find—"

He kissed me hard and slid inside the cabin, gently pushing me back. With the heel of his boot, he shut the door behind him. I was lost in the kiss as his tongue explored my mouth and his hands roamed my body with an urgency that weakened my knees. His hands were working on the buttons of my shirt. Yes! My legs touched the bed. A moment later, I was lying on it with Rennie on top of me.

"I can't fight it anymore," he whispered, tracing my jaw with his lips. "But if you want me to leave, just say it."

"No." I gripped his biceps. "Don't leave."

A sinful smirk twitched his lips. He kissed me again, one hand cupping my breast. The hard length of his erection rubbed exactly where I wanted it to, but it only made me wilder. He scattered kisses on my neck while undoing my shirt. When his hot mouth closed around my nipple, I arched my back, begging for more. A jolt of desire went through me when he slipped a hand under my skirt.

His deft fingers were so close to my throbbing nub. I sighed as he sucked my nipple gently. His shaven chin... shaven? I remembered feeling his stubble earlier. He could have shaved meanwhile, but the smell of the after-shave cologne he used was missing.

I froze, my eyes flaring open. Oh, no. Oh. No. "You aren't Rennie."

He lifted his head, and for a terrible split second, his pupils became two vertical slits and his eyes turned black.

I screamed. I couldn't help it. Yes, it was pretty useless. I should have hit him in the bollocks, although I had no idea if such a move would hurt a lamia. But at that moment, freezing and screaming sounded like a jolly good idea.

He froze too, as if confused. "Stop screaming."

"Let me go!" I shoved him... it. But it didn't budge.

"Stop it."

The door to my cabin was flung open, and Rennie, the real one, barged inside. There was a moment of chilled silence during which we remained still, watching each other. Then Rennie grabbed the lamia by the shoulders and hurled it away. With shaky fingers, I buttoned my shirt and adjusted my skirt. They fought, rolling on the floor, with their identical grey jackets flapping around. I snatched the oil lamp from the nightstand and lifted my arm, ready to strike... but who? Confound it. Who was the real Rennie?

"Hit him!" one of the two yelled.

But what if he was the wrong one? From here, I couldn't see Rennie's stubble.

"Monia, hit him!" the other one said.

Oh, blast it. I shifted my weight as Rennie One punched Rennie Two in the temple. I didn't know if I should cheer or despair. Rennie One straddled Rennie Two and rained punches on his face. Groans and grunts filled the room.

"Monia!" Rennie Two, the one being punched, said.

"Lawrence?" I called, taken by a sudden inspiration.

Rennie Two nodded. "It's me."

A thud ricocheted off the walls when I smashed the oil lamp onto the nape of Rennie One. His eyes rolled back into his skull, and he dropped to the floor in a heap of limbs.

"Ha! Take that!" I smiled at Rennie. "I knew you would have answered if I'd called you Lawrence."

Rennie's eyes flashed black, the colour of onyx. "Thank you, darling." He sprang up and darted out of the room, which meant the unconscious Rennie on the floor was the real one. And I had bludgeoned him into oblivion.

Oops.

I crouched next to him and brushed his hair from his bruised face. "Rennie, please say something."

He didn't stir. I touched his neck. His heartbeat was slow but steady. I took the basin of water and cleaned the blood from his face. A lump was clogging my throat.

"Rennie?" Fear drummed in my chest. I was about to call the doctor when he blinked and groaned.

"Hellfire." He rubbed his face.

Relief washed over me. I knelt next to him and took his hand. "I'm so sorry."

"My head."

"I know, I know." I put the wet cloth on his nape.

"Bloody hell, woman. You knocked me out."

"I thought the other one was the real Rennie when I called him Lawrence and he answered."

He shot me a glare. No lamia could imitate that look. "I was in the middle of a fight. Why would I reply if you called me Lawrence?"

"I didn't know what to do, all right? We should discuss a watchword, something that will identify you."

He sat up, groaning. "I almost caught it."

"Sorry."

He waved a dismissive hand. "I'm grateful you didn't kill me." Rubbing the back of his neck, he eyed the bed. "Were you and the lamia...?"

Heat flushed my face, which was ridiculous. Rennie

and I had enjoyed some intimate moments, but being caught doing the same things with someone else caused my chest to tighten in shame.

"Well, a bit. I thought it was you. I did wonder, though, why you wanted to have a proper fumble right in the middle of the day." I cleared my throat. "Admittedly, I didn't question that part much. I was too enthralled by the activity."

He chuckled, his chest rising and falling quickly. "Was it any good?"

"No!" I wiped more blood from his chin. "Something was missing. You are inimitable. Unique. My only one."

His smile vanished. "Am I? Your only one?"

I caressed his cheek. "You are."

Holding my hand, he kissed my wrist. "So are you. You have wrapped me around your little finger."

"Not as much as I'd like, since you don't want to have a proper fumble with me."

"Who says I don't want to? It's only the bloody work that keeps me away from you. Speaking of which. Sorry it took me so long. I left the ship to send a wire to the bureau." He kissed my wrist again. "Apparently, Oliver has a hefty debt due to some unwise financial investments. The man Oliver met in Bellini Garden is most likely an Unnatural smuggler, willing to pay Oliver a large sum of money for the lamia."

I sat back, shocked by the fact a man like Oliver, who was supposed to protect innocent people, was selling

Unnaturals. "How awful." I dabbed another cut on Rennie's chin.

I shifted next to him on the floor. My arm was sore after I'd used all my strength to hit Rennie. If it hadn't been for the shaven chin, I would have left the lamia to keep going. The devil was in the details. The lamia should have known Rennie had stubble today. The last time his cheeks had been shaven was when we—"Oh, my gosh. I think I know where the lamia is."

SEVENTEEN

IF THE ENGINE room smelled of oil and coal dust, the cargo hold smelled like a pair of socks after a four-hour ride.

All sorts of supplies were stored in the belly of the ship, from kitchen provisions to passengers' items too big to be kept in the cabin. If my theory was correct, the lamia should be nestled here. The last time we'd been searching the cargo hold, Rennie's chin had been perfectly shaven. If the lamia had seen him and copied his style, then it meant its nest should be around. Yes, it was a deuced feeble thread, but I didn't have any other ideas.

Rennie walked in front of me on the balls of his feet to be quiet. He needn't have bothered though. Noises rumbled in the packed space. There were metallic groans that made me worry the ship was going to be split in half, and dull thuds, like air pressed inside a pipe. I jolted every time steam hissed from a valve. Our oil lamps were the only source of light. I released a breath when we arrived at a silent portion of the hold, my ears throbbing from their previous misuse.

"We've checked this place quite a few times," Rennie said. "I'm not sure we'll find anything."

"We've checked the *entire* ship quite a few times. Yet the lamia must be somewhere."

"Fair point, Miss Fitzwilliam."

"Thank you, Lawrence."

He flashed me a cheeky grin that, in better circumstances, would have distracted me. After an hour of creeping along narrow passages and smelling buckets of onions, my morale wasn't so optimistic any longer. Perhaps my idea was nonsense. I plonked down onto a wooden crate filled with potatoes, according to the label.

"I'm ready to admit defeat," I said, throwing a hand up.

Sighing, Rennie sat next to me. "It was worth a try."

As we remained silent, a soft, chirping noise reached my ears. I gazed around.

"Are there birds trapped down here? Poor things." I rose and focused on the muffled noise.

"Birds? I don't hear anything."

"Shush." I tilted my head.

The chirping came from my left where piles of fruit were stacked. I went to rush in that direction, but Rennie grabbed my arm.

"Wait," he said.

"What?"

"What if it's a trick of the lamia?"

A sudden chill crawled up my neck. "Let's have a look," I said.

"I'm not sure it's a good idea."

The chirping came again, sad and painful, as if the beasts were desperate or hungry.

"Just a peek." I shrugged free and tiptoed closer to the noise.

It took a bit of rummaging through mysterious boxes and crates of dried fruit before I found it. It was a nest. It emitted a faint white glow and was made from pieces of straw. Inside it, there were the most adorable, fluffy creatures I'd ever seen, something between a white kitten and a tiny bunny. Large blue eyes stared up at me. Pink button noses sniffed the air, and rounded ears twitched. Tiny paws clawed the air.

"Oh, my goodness." My heart melted at the sight of those little balls of fur. There were five of them. "What are they?"

"Bloody hell." Rennie scratched the back of his neck. "They look like bloody kittens."

"They're so cute."

Footsteps padded behind us. We both spun around. The lamia, in the form of Rennie's hideous tutor, walked towards us, its nostrils flaring and its eyes turning fully black.

"Do not touch them," it hissed.

Rennie's hand slipped under his jacket where his gun was sheathed. A lump swelled in my throat at the thought of harming those lovely darlings.

I held up my hands. "We don't want to hurt them."

"They might be lovely now, but they will grow into killers," Rennie said.

"I do not kill." The lamia's upper lip curled in a snarl, showing sharp teeth.

"You killed Mrs Francis." Rennie's gun made an appearance. "We never found her body because you destroyed it."

The lamia's body shivered, his features blurring before returning sharp. "She died because of a seizure. She wanted to be alone with her Scottish lover. I feed on people's dreams and fears, not on their flesh. But the love-making was too much for her, and she died. I merely destroyed her body."

I put a hand on Rennie's arm before he cocked the hammer. "And why do you follow me?" I asked the lamia.

Its body morphed into Rennie's when I stared at its eyes. Now that I noticed them, they were a darker shade of green than my Rennie's. "You've been bitten by an earth eel and survived. Not many humans can say that."

Even the voice was identical to Rennie's.

"What does that mean?" I asked, intrigued.

"Your dreams are the best food for my babies because your emotions are strong." Its gaze flickered towards the white bunnies. "Don't hurt them." There was a desperate note now in its voice, and the fact it looked and sounded like Rennie made my chest constrict with sorrow.

"The bureau has evidence lamiae have killed humans," Rennie insisted.

Lamia-Rennie shook its head. "Natural deaths. I told you I don't eat flesh. I feed on dreams, bad and good, the more vivid, the better. The human must be alive for me to feed."

"I believe it," I said.

"Monia," Rennie started, and I didn't like how he said my name, as if I were being unreasonable. "Unnaturals can't be trusted, especially when they have babies to protect."

"Babies? My word, now, that's something interesting." Oliver stepped into our suddenly busy little space.

The lamia hissed and changed into a beautiful woman with long, wavy red hair. Oliver's past lover, perhaps? His mother? Whoever she was, he paled, his jaw twitching.

"You're an agent, Rennie," he said. "Your duty is to catch this Unnatural and its babies."

Rennie pointed his gun at Oliver. "Trafficking Unnaturals is against the law."

"You're right." Oliver took another step closer. "Then shoot the lamia and kill those babies. Be brave and do it."

A gasp remained trapped in my mouth. I gave Rennie a pleading glance. If the lamia had told the truth, it was innocent, and its babies shouldn't be killed. Non-threatening Unnaturals should be protected rather than killed. The tendons in Rennie's neck throbbed as he kept his gun trained on Oliver.

"I'm arresting and reporting you to the bureau for document forgery and trafficking Unnaturals." He shifted to shield the babies from Oliver's angry sight. "And no one is going to hurt those furry babies."

At his words, something warm burst within my chest and spread through my body. I already knew he was a kind, honourable man, but at that moment, watching him ready to protect those little creatures, all my affection for him flared. I wanted to hug him and kiss him until we were both breathless. I wanted to tell him how much I cared about him. I wanted to be with him forever.

"Don't worry, Rennie, Monia," Oliver said. "I will tell your families how tragically the lamia attacked and killed both of you."

As I was lost in my sweet thoughts about Rennie being a caring and loving man, Oliver lunged. Rennie fell backwards. The noise of a shot ricocheted off the walls. I jolted back. The kittens-bunnies gave a terrified squeal, and the lamia rushed towards them. It dispensed with the human form and turned into a white ball of fur, beautiful and fluffy just like the babies, only bigger. It was a pitiful sight, the terrified Unnatural curled around its babies, shivering with its pupils dilated and hissing in fear.

I wouldn't stay here and do nothing. So I jumped on Oliver's back and grabbed his neck and... if I was being honest, I wasn't sure what I wanted to do next. Instinct was guiding me, which, admittedly, might not be a clever thing. But I'd never been trained to fight. I was a champion at needlework, though. No one could embroider a quilt faster than I could. I'd actually won a cross-stitching competition.

And I wasn't bad on a horse either as long as the horse was good-natured, the weather fine, and the path easy.

Oliver grunted in annoyance when I squeezed my arms hard around his neck. Beneath him, Rennie was struggling to free himself from Oliver's grip. I squeezed harder, feeling the roped muscles in Oliver's neck tensing. Another bullet swished past me, startling me and causing me to release my grip.

Pain hit my chest. Something warm, sticky, and red trickled down my body. Sheer fear chilled me to the bones. I'd been shot. With a push, Rennie shoved Oliver, who fell to the floor, and rushed towards me. His green eyes were wide with worry as he crouched next to me.

"Re-Rennie," I croaked out, pressing my hand against my chest. "I'm dying."

"But—"

"I don't think I have much time." My voice sounded rasping, but I had to talk. "I love you."

His mouth dropped open as he held my hand. "Monia."

I let out a long exhalation, burning pain bothering my throat. "I can die now. I just had to tell you how I feel. Please, remember me, my love. I would've loved you forever. You're the best man I've ever met. There. Now I can leave you."

He chuckled, which I didn't like because I wanted my predicament to be taken seriously. I was dying, for Pete's sake, and trying to make the most of my last moments on

Earth. I glowered, which made him laugh harder. Honestly.

"It's not blood, sweetheart. A jar of tomato sauce crashed, and the contents dropped on you." He caressed my cheek, tears glistening in the corners of his eyes. "Oliver was hit, not you. He grabbed the gun, but then he fell on top of it, shooting himself."

"Oh." I touched my chest and glanced down at the bright red stain. Admittedly, the smell should have made me think. "Are you sure?"

"Very."

"I feel pain in my chest."

"Because the jar hit you."

"Well." I tipped my chin up, gathering all the dignity I could muster. "I guess I'm all right then."

He bent over me and kissed my lips. "And I love you, too."

EIGHTEEN

KEEPING HIDDEN A man's body on a cruise ship wasn't an easy task. We couldn't simply throw Oliver overboard. That would be horrible, even though he was a scoundrel. Not to mention we could be spotted doing the deed. We couldn't let a body decompose in the cargo hold, and we couldn't ask the captain to please moor somewhere so we could dump Oliver in a ditch.

The SS *Florentia* was sailing towards Ibiza under a shiny turquoise sky but in a strong gale. Due to bad sea conditions, it was taking longer than usual to reach the Spanish island. We were going to be stuck with a corpse for days. Also, there was no Royal Occult Bureau in Ibiza, and it would be hard to explain to the Spanish Unnatural Office what had happened.

The only reasonable solution was to let the lamia do its body-vanishing trick, as it'd done with poor Mrs Francis.

Rennie didn't have the power to cleanse people's memories. If someone saw Oliver's body, we would be arrested.

The lamia wrapped around Oliver's body, its fur expanding and shining. Nauseating noises, like bones breaking and flesh being cut, resonated as the lamia emitted a faint silver light. Despite the glittering glow and the little silver stars shining around, it wasn't a pretty sight. I turned around, trying to wipe the tomato sauce from my shirt with a handkerchief. It was a useless task. I would have more success dusting the Sahara.

Rennie draped his jacket around my shoulders, covering the stain. "As soon as we reach Ibiza, we must wire the bureau. After that, do you want to go back home?"

I peered at the lamia who was finishing its job. "What about the lamia?"

Rennie scrubbed his chin, staring at the lovely babies watching us with big, terrified eyes. "I think we should leave the lamia alone."

I wrapped my arms around his neck and kissed him on the mouth. "Will the bureau be a problem?"

He held me by the waist. "I'll write a report and explain to my superiors the lamia isn't an extremely dangerous creature. It does need regulation, since it can scare people to death, but it's not a killer. Protection laws are very clear about which Unnaturals should be exterminated or restrained. It might take a bit of work, but I'm confident that with the help of some of my co-workers, we can build a solid case in favour of the lamia."

I kissed him again, pressing my body against his. He

broke the kiss, eyes shining with lust. "Not here, luv, not next to Oliver's melted body and a litter of furry babies."

Yes, five pairs of innocent eyes stared at us. Mommy lamia coiled around its babies and gave us a nod, as if thanking us. I waved and smiled, and the babies let out cute cooing sounds.

"Let's go then." I took his hand before he could protest and dragged him out of the cargo hold.

RENNIE'S SOFT CHUCKLE echoed down the narrow staircase that led us to the upper deck.

"I'm not sure why you're laughing," I said. "Because I'm very serious about what I want to do to you."

"Oh, sweetheart."

I liked it when he called me that. As we strode along the first-class corridor, I closed my hand around his. Breathless, I stopped in front of my cabin and fiddled with the key.

"Monia." He tugged at my hand. I preferred when he called me sweetheart. "Perhaps we should wait."

"Shut up. It's the best idea I've ever had."

"Your parents—"

"They aren't here." Thank goodness. "And I need help to remove my clothes," I added in a whisper.

Instant heat flushed through his gaze. "I would gladly help. But—"

"Great." I pushed the door open and yanked him inside none-too-gently.

He remained next to the door, hands in his pockets. "The fact the lamia and Oliver aren't a danger anymore doesn't mean the contract I signed is null."

"We won't tell anyone." I removed his jacket.

"That's the point. I want to tell everyone. I want your parents to know about us and to give us their blessing."

My mother would never do that, and I was tired of waiting. So I undid the first buttons of my shirt. "Can you help me here?" I sashayed towards him.

His gaze flickered over the triangle of skin left bare by the shirt. He undid a few other buttons. The hem of my chemise was visible now.

"Is that all right?" he asked.

I shook my head. "I still need help."

He unfastened two other buttons, revealing the top of my breasts.

"More buttons," I whispered.

He obliged, but I didn't miss the worried expression on his face. I wanted him to stop thinking about my parents, mostly because if he thought of them, I'd think of them too, and it was a major distraction from my seductive plan.

When he unfastened the last button, I wriggled out of the shirt without thinking too much. Before he could say anything, I removed my chemise as well. I was standing half-naked in front of him. Better to remove my skirts as well. It looked too odd to stay with my breasts bare and my legs clothed.

Right when I was wrestling myself out of my petticoats, the ship decided it was a good moment to jolt. I lost my balance and staggered to the left. Rennie's arms curled around me before I could hit the floor. His chest rose, and his nostrils flared. I waited for him to either finish what we —well, I'd started, or to blather some nonsense about the contract.

He ripped my skirts with a big yank, then he dropped me to the bed and kissed me hard and deeply. He paused only to brush my hair from my face. "There is no going back after this."

I nodded, although I wasn't completely sure what he meant. But he sucked at my nipple while tweaking the other, and any rational thought left my mind. His hand ran up and down my body as he kissed his way to my navel and thighs.

Heaven. I liked that so much. The first lash of his tongue shot so much pleasure to my brain I was worried it might burst. He held my legs wide apart with his rough hands while he plunged his tongue between my folds and deep inside me. His fingers joined the game, sliding in and out of me and rubbing my little nub. It was an assault of fingers, tongue, lips, and teeth. Now and then, his fingers rubbed my nipples, making me moan and jolt with pleasure.

I came with a start, his name leaving my lips with a scream. He didn't stop but kept licking and kissing me. Soon, I was squirming again, but he paused just long enough to remove his trousers and shirt. I had barely time to admire his sculpted body and the sharp ridges of his defined abdominal muscles before his shaft brushed against my entrance.

Breathing hard, he remained still, his muscles taut with tension. "Are you sure?"

"Do it. I want it. I want you."

He slid an inch inside me.

My inner muscles, still dizzy after the release, stretched almost painfully. Propped on his elbows, Rennie inched onwards, making me feel exactly how big he was. I bunched the bed sheets under my fists and rolled my hips, meeting his length. The more he thrust, the more my flesh burned, but the pain was manageable, and the sensation of him stretching me started a flutter of butterflies in my belly.

When he was fully inside me, he waited before starting to move in and out. Each time he entered me a bit harder, went a bit deeper. The tip of his shaft hit just the right spot inside me to make me squirm. Rennie kissed me, biting my bottom lip and then sucking it into his velvety mouth. His pace became faster, and his kisses more hungry. Quick breaths came out of his mouth as he thrust in and out of me. The pain vanished, replaced only by the head-spinning pleasure of him stretching me. Energy built up again. Another release detonated through my body. I bent my knees while he kept his punishing rhythm. Breathing hard, he pulled out of me to spill onto the bed. I lay exhausted, my body a bundle of emotions, sore and sated, filled with love.

"Oh, Rennie."

He took a cloth and wiped me, the bed, and himself. Desire darkened his gaze. "We haven't finished yet."

His mouth closed around my extremely sensitive nipple and sucked at it while his fingers stroked my even more sensitive folds and nub. He massaged me gently, sliding a finger inside now and then. I didn't think my body would respond to his ministrations after the last release, but soon wetness pooled between my thighs again. As if sensing it, he pinched my nipple hard before dipping his face between my legs. He wasn't gentle. He ate me with a ferocious hunger that shot thrills up my back. Then he started it all over again, tonguing my nipples and thrusting his fingers deep inside me.

When he flipped me onto my belly, I wondered what he wanted to do. But he kissed my nub again before slamming inside me from behind. In that position, his shaft reached a far deeper spot within my tender flesh. He didn't stop pumping in and out of me until he extracted two more releases from my overly responsive body.

My word, I had no idea it was possible.

He curled around me, protecting me with his strong arms and lulling me into sleep.

I woke up the next morning wonderfully sore and with Rennie's arms around me. I lost count of how many times he'd taken me during the night. His shaft must be supernatural because every single time he entered me, my body ignited in a burst of pleasure.

WE SPENT THE next two days in bed, making love, sleeping, and watching the baby lamiae grow.

My parents were waiting for us in Ibiza, and with each mile we sailed closer to the island, a weight pressed against my chest. Rennie wanted to talk to them, tell them everything, including that he wanted to court me. I had at least ten better ideas that involved eloping and riding off together in the sunset on a docile horse, of course. Rennie didn't show the enthusiasm I would have liked to see. I barely paid attention to Ibiza's turquoise sea, white rocks, and palm trees as Rennie and I walked hand in hand towards the hotel where my parents had a room.

Mother hugged me. Father shook hands with Rennie. It took us a while to tell them about Oliver and the lamia. My parents' pride for me brought tears to my eyes. Then Father and I went to the telegraph office to send a wire to London's Royal Occult Bureau while Rennie and my mother locked themselves in a room. She was the one he had to convince.

The fresh scent of the sea lifted my mood as Father and I strolled along the narrow, cobbled streets of Ibiza Town. The white walls of the houses reflected the bright sunlight. Pots of red geraniums and roses overflowed the balconies and window sills. If it weren't for the weight pressing against my chest, it'd be a beautiful view.

"I imagine Rennie doesn't want to talk to your mother about the lamia, am I right?" Father said.

"Yes, you are." My cheeks flamed.

He patted my hand. "Do you care about him?" The sweet tone in his voice caused my heart to flutter.

"Yes, and he cares about me."

"I like him. I think he's a brave man with a good heart, but your mother won't be happy about having him as her son-in-law."

My mood plummeted to the ground. The people in colourful dresses and the songs didn't lift it. "Can't you convince her?"

"She wants only the best for you."

"Can't I decide what's best for me?" There was more venom in my voice than I meant.

Father gazed down. "After the incident, your mother blamed herself for having allowed you to come with us. At first, she thought travelling with us would make you stronger and more knowledgeable. But after the incident, she was terrified. She hated watching you have nightmares. She meant well. And I supported her because I was scared about your health, too. We want to protect you, darling."

"But I want Rennie, Papa, with all my heart. He's the man I want to spend the rest of my life with."

We stopped in the middle of a pavement made of colourful cobblestones. Each one glimmered with a different colour.

Father released a breath. "As long as you're happy, I don't care whom you want to marry."

I hugged him, inhaling the scent of tobacco. "Thank you, Papa."

When I returned to the hotel, Mother's stern, pale face said everything I needed to know. Rennie's jaw was locked.

I swallowed hard. The air in the hotel room was as thick and frosty as a glacier. "Mother—"

"Monia, this nonsense ends here. You're going back to England with us," she said.

I closed my fists into tight balls. "I want to be with Rennie, Mother. This isn't nonsense. It's my life."

"If you insist on following this path, then I'll be forced to apply the legal power of the contract and have Rennie arrested. Come home with us, and Rennie walks free."

Rennie gazed at the floor, hands in his pockets. I was sure he had a lot to say, but it was a conversation I had to take care of personally.

Shock stunned me into silence for a moment charged with anger. "You're blackmailing me."

"I want you to understand the huge mistake you're about to make."

"Laura," Papa said, stepping next to me. "Monia loves Rennie, and he loves her. You must take that into consideration."

"Her safety comes before anything else." Mother's voice shook. "What will happen if she marries an occult agent? Her life will always be in danger. We've already risked her safety one too many times."

"Mother—"

"Enough!" Her voice rose with a hysterical note of panic. "You're returning home with us. I'll let the contract go if you come without a fuss."

Rennie glanced at me and gave me a nod while mouthing, "I love you."

Blazes. I didn't want him to be tortured or imprisoned because of me. My shoulders sagged as my eyes filled with tears. "I will return home with you."

EPILOGUE

THREE MONTHS LATER

IT TOOK TWO months for the baby lamiae to grow into adulthood.

I'd taken them with me, both because I wanted to protect them and because it annoyed Mother. Also, the bureau had still to decide how to deal with the lamiae, but I wouldn't let anyone hurt them. Hence their presence in my room.

Three months had passed since the last time I'd seen Rennie, and my heart had never stopped aching. I missed him so much that the lamiae kept turning into him. So now I had six Rennies in my bedroom—mama lamia and her babies. But the original was the only one that mattered.

I'd begged, argued, and yelled at Mother, but she didn't care. She kept saying she was doing the right thing for me and my future. There was no future without

Rennie. That was why I was going to leave my house and live my life. Now that the lamiae were adults and didn't need me anymore, I was ready to go. A part of me wished that Mother would see reason. I'd given her plenty of time to think about her horrible attitude. Enough was enough. I was going to claim my man, and to hell with it.

I had no reason to stay at my parents' house. I would leave, find Rennie, and elope.

The door to my bedroom was flung open, and Mother strode inside the room. The lamiae disappeared, turning into tiny globes of light that could barely be spotted.

Her hair was dishevelled, and her eyes were wide. "Monia!"

I stood up. "Is something the matter? Is Father all right?"

"I have realised I made a mistake," she said, stepping closer. Her cheeks were flushed.

"I beg your pardon."

"I've made a mistake," she repeated.

"Are you drunk?"

"How dare you?" Anger caused her expression to return to normal. She was less wild, her steely gaze on me. "I'm simply trying to admit my mistakes. The fear of losing you made me blind." A tear glistened in the corner of her eye. "But I've realised the fear of making you unhappy was greater. You have my blessing, child. You can marry your Rennie."

My mouth dropped open. "Oh, Mother."

She wrung her hands. "I hope you'll forgive me. I thought I was protecting you."

"Of course, I forgive you." I swallowed the lump in my throat. "What made you change your mind?"

Her gaze darted around. "Well, a few things. A few thoughts."

The explanation was rather vague. But I didn't care. I hugged her, and she hugged me back, kissing my forehead. "Don't elope, darling. I want you to have a proper wedding, with the banns of marriage, a silk dress, and lots of flowers. A beautiful wedding like the one I had."

"Of course. I'd be delighted."

"Good." She kissed my forehead again before smiling, but not at me. She was staring at a point behind me. "I'll leave you alone then." She chuckled when she said 'alone.'

What in the name of Hades had just happened?

With a series of popping sounds, the lamiae turned into my personal team of Rennies, wearing identical suits and smirks.

"I knew it would work," Rennie One said, sliding an arm around my waist.

"What have you done?" I asked none of them in particular.

Rennie Two lifted a shoulder. "We showed your mother a few of her most intimate fears until she understood she was going to lose you if you weren't happy."

Rennie Three took my face and kissed my lips. "Why don't we celebrate your imminent engagement with some wild fumbles?"

That was another good thing about the lamiae imitating Rennie. They used exactly the words I wanted to hear because I doubted my Rennie would have said something like that. Rennie Three kissed me hard and slipped his tongue between my lips.

I withdrew and shook my head. "Uh-uh. You know the rules. No lovemaking. I want only the real Rennie."

"Just a kiss." He followed me, and his lips were on mine again, demanding and dominant.

I put a hand on his chest. "We shouldn't—"

His hand grabbed my breast and kneaded it, brushing his thumb over my nipple until I moaned. Dash it, it felt so good. But it wasn't the real Rennie.

"I mean it." I gazed around. The other Rennies were smiling around me, all seven of them... seven? Yes, there were seven. Since when did I have seven Rennies in my bedroom? "Lawrence?" The breath was punched out of me.

"The one and only." He wrapped my arms around my waist, beaming.

"But, how?"

"You didn't think I would let you go without a fight, did you? Mother lamia and I became friends, well, more or less. It slipped out of your bedroom at night to see me. It helped me train its puppies to show your mother how wrong her attitude was. I know how important your family is to you. I wanted your mother to admit she was wrong on her own. It took a while, but here I am."

"How did you enter my bedroom without me noticing?"

He arched a brow. "Seriously? I'm an occult agent."

I had other questions, but confound it, we had time to talk in the future. I took his face and brought it down for a burning kiss, making him feel all the passion and desire I felt. He kissed me back, caressing my body with his big hands.

"I've missed you so much," he whispered, kissing my neck. "And I'll show you just how much."

As the lamiae did their dissolving trick and went somewhere else, he laid me on the bed and started undoing my shirt. "I'm going to feast on you until you come, screaming my name."

I grinned. Lord, what a splendid plan.

THE END

FANCY A REVIEW? YES!

Thank you so much for reading Monia and Rennie's story. I hope you enjoyed it as much as I enjoyed writing it. If you liked it, please, please, PLEASE leave a review here:

http://www.amazon.com/review/create-review?&asin=

The review doesn't need to be long. Just 'I enjoyed it' is enough.

Thank you!

ABOUT ME

Love stories have always captured my imagination. What's better than two people falling in love with each other? I write steamy romance, usually with a paranormal twist in an historical setting. Add a touch of suspense and mystery and a pinch of darkness. I love stories with strong, sexy heroes and mischievous heroines who pull no punches.

I live in the City of Sails, New Zealand, drinking tea (coffee gives me anxiety) and devouring books.

Join my newsletter for exclusive content and the chance to receive an ARC copy of my books. Just copy and paste this link into your browser:

Barbara's Newsletter: https://bit.ly/39yZ4Lw

If you love steamy paranormal romance set in Victorian London, my Royal Occult Bureau series is for you:
The Royal Occult Bureau Series

For Victorian historical romance, check out my Victorian Outcasts series:
Victorian Outcasts

Are you into shape-shifter romance? Check out my da Vinci's Beasts series, set in WW2:
da Vinci's Beasts Series

For more Victorian paranormal romance with witches and sexy warriors, see the Knights of the White Blade series:
The White Order Series

ALSO BY BARBARA RUSSELL

The Royal Occult Bureau

The Royal Occult Bureau

Quicksilver

The Beat of a Man's Heart

The Kiss Thief

On the Origin of Unnatural Species

By the Pricking of My Thumbs

Mrs Lynch

A Gloomy Shade of Death

Kiss of Steele

Victorian Outcasts

Taming the Savage Duke

The Earl's Red Hot Wedding

The Wrath of the Marquess

The Viscount's Marriage of Inconvenience

The Baron Who Never Danced

Lord Ravenscroft is Not a Gentleman

The King of Whitechapel

The White Order

The Pact of the White Blade Knights
The Fire of the White Blade Knights
The Spirit of the White Blade Knights
Captain Sancerre
The Beauty of the White Blade Knights
The Vengeance of the White Blade Knights

da Vinci's Beasts

If I Were Fire
If I Were Wind
If I Were Water
If I Were the Maker (Coming soon)—da Vinci's Beasts#4

Stand alone

Butterfly—steamy contemporary romance
Between the King and His Wrath

www.ingramcontent.com/pod-product-compliance
Ingram Content Group UK Ltd.
Pitfield, Milton Keynes, MK11 3LW, UK
UKHW030730240225
455493UK00005B/413